The
King
of Hearts'
Heart

The King of Hearts' Heart

by
Sam Teague

Little, Brown and Company
Boston   Toronto

First Edition

Library of Congress Cataloging-in-Publication Data
Teague, Sam.
  The king of hearts' heart.

  Summary: Aspiring to make the varsity track team, thirteen-year-
old Harold neglects his brain-damaged friend Billy until a crisis
leads him to transfer his dreams of championship to Billy.
  [1. Brain-damaged children—Fiction.   2. Mentally
handicapped—Fiction.   3. Track and field—Fiction.
4. Friendship—Fiction]   I. Title.
PZ7.T219383Ki 1987   [Fic]   86-27484
ISBN 0-316-83427-0

Designed by Trisha Hanlon

RRD–VA

Published simultaneously in Canada
by Little, Brown & Company (Canada) Limited
Printed in the United States of America

For Hope and Tobey
and four special critics:
Kate, Bill, Robert, and Bruce

The
King
of Hearts'
Heart

Chapter 1

Billy has always lived next door to me. We were born the same month in the same hospital, and there was less than an ounce difference in our weights at birth. Although I was a few days older, Billy was the first to talk and the first to walk, and he was potty trained a full two months before I stopped smelling up our neighborhood.

The first four years of our lives are pressed together in Mom's blue photo album: a hundred color snapshots of Billy and me, a hundred different stories. There are pictures of Billy pulling me in my wagon, Billy helping me up the steps, Billy lacing and tying my shoes. There are pictures of me holding Billy's hand, me following Billy's lead, me hugging Billy's neck.

I don't remember some of the pictures being taken, but Mom remembers everything about them: dates, seasons, and circumstances. One day every December Mom cancels all my afternoon activities and spends three hours sitting on the sofa with me at her side and the blue photo album in our laps, discussing every photograph Billy and I had shared those first four years. At the end of the session she closes the album, takes my face in her hands, and whispers in a voice as warm as my feelings toward Billy at that moment: "Be ye kind, one to another, Harold. It could have been you."

It could have been me. The accident happened in the early part of our fourth December together. Billy and I were swinging on the old tire that hung from the oak tree in his front yard. We stood facing each other on top of the tire and gripped the rope so tightly that it left its patterned imprint across the palms of our hands. We pumped our legs, and the tire swing sailed toward heaven. Back and forth it went, higher and higher, pausing for a second up in the air before falling through space like a runaway roller coaster, and taking our breath away as it raced toward earth.

I remember Billy's laughter as the swing hesitated high above the spot where the sidewalk buckled beneath us, its jagged edges split open, waiting openmouthed like a shark for its prey. Suddenly Billy lost his balance, or I lost mine. I don't remember who slipped first, and it never really mattered except on the rainy days when I thumbed through Mom's blue photo album. What mattered was that the tire swing jerked spasmodically with the first loss of balance, and its riders fell pell-mell into nothingness.

We dropped twenty feet to the ground. I landed flat on my rear on the grass at the edge of the sidewalk and scratched my finger on a small twig. Billy, however, fell full force on his head, right into the shark's mouth.

I remember the blood. It kept coming, kept spilling from Billy's head onto the sidewalk, where I can see stains in the cement even now. Straddling my friend, I pulled open his eyelids and stared into his blank blue eyes. I cupped my hands over the wound, and as his warm blood seeped into my scratch and between my fingers, I begged Billy not to die.

Billy didn't die, but he didn't wake up for three weeks. Within that space of time, Billy's life was changed forever. The day after Santa had dropped off Billy's toys, they were too old for him. My neighbor and first friend had suffered brain damage, and in the time it took to rock a tire swing, he was forever mentally retarded. It had all started with our fall, and it could have been me.

Now, nine years later, Billy and I were no longer the picture-perfect playmates we had been before that Christmas. When I was six my parents tried to explain that my friend had stayed behind to live a little longer as a four-year-old. The gap in our mental ages widened with time. When I was eight, Billy was six. And by the time we turned twelve, it seemed as though we were worlds apart. Since we were still neighbors, we were still friends, but distant ones; I had other friends and interests now, and even when Billy and I did things together, we weren't necessarily together. For instance, we seldom sat in the same row at the movies, not even the scary ones. (Billy would sit directly in front of me, which made it easy to keep an eye on him without having to listen to all his questions.)

Billy embarrassed me with a regularity that kept my face flush and my cheeks warm, and it amazed me that neither Billy's parents nor mine were ever embarrassed by his slow mind and quick actions. They were not even embarrassed at the church program when Billy sang "Jesus Loves Me" to the entire congregation, towering a full three heads above the heads of the other Happy Faces Choir members, singing a full octave below them, and beaming as though he were responsible for the naming of the choir. Billy could not carry a tune in the seat of his baggy pants, but everyone congratulated him anyway.

"Billy sang beautifully tonight," his mom said as my dad drove all of us home.

"You could hear Billy's lovely voice over all the others," Mom commented, and I bit my lower lip to keep from laughing aloud. Then she said, "Wouldn't it be nice if Harold volunteered to take Billy skating Friday night?" and I bit my lower lip to keep from crying aloud.

Volunteer? I knew what that meant—I'd have no choice in the matter. But not this time, I told myself. Lecture or no lecture, I wasn't going to volunteer. "But Billy can't skate," I said, glancing toward the front seat of the station wagon and noting Dad's wrinkled nose in the rearview mirror.

"You could help him, Harold," Mom said.

"Don't you remember what happened last time?" I asked.

"You *will* take Billy skating Friday night, Harold," Dad's nose said, and I volunteered.

Chapter 2

Skating with Billy. I'll remember it when I have kids my age. It was Friday night, the night I had decided to make Kate Miller fall in love with me.

Kate Miller had transferred to Lakeside Junior High from a school across town, and the second she walked into my seventh-grade science class, I was in love. Had I kept a list of my favorite things in the world prior to Kate Miller, the list would have consisted of running track, roller skating, Snickers, and girls; and girls would have only recently made the list. Before Kate Miller, sexual matters had disturbed my thoughts very little, unless you count the magazines that Tim Martin had found under his father's bed and had sneaked into the boys' locker room. But Tim's pictures didn't count, because they were only pictures. Kate Miller was not a picture. She was a Patti Bannister painting.

She was beautiful. She had long chestnut hair that fell halfway down her back, a perfect complexion, dark eyes, full lips, and breasts. Real breasts. Not large breasts like the ones in Tim's magazines, but breasts that actually protruded from her chest like a baby's knuckles protruded from a smooth, clenched fist. It was my good fortune that Larry Johnson and I had been separated earlier for talking during class, and the only vacant desk was Larry's old one to my left. Kate Miller and her breasts took their places next to me.

A week passed, and Kate never noticed me. Two weeks passed, and she continued to act as if I didn't exist. She seemed totally oblivious to the pencils, pens, papers, and books that crashed from my desk to the floor of the aisle between us. I began to wonder if I had bad breath or body odor. Worse, I began to question my mother's laundry habits: was my underwear clean or did Mom simply pretend to wash it? My life was getting out of control. I gained four pounds from breath mints, my body reeked with Dad's after-shave, I stopped wearing underwear altogether, and I developed a tender chafe between my thighs. I suffered because of Kate Miller. My mother thought I was ill; my father said it was a phase; my mother decided I was weird; my father agreed with her.

But it was worth everything. One Friday, at the close of the unit on anatomy, Kate Miller picked up a bruised pencil I had rolled from my desk. "I heard you can skate," she said.

"I'm okay," I managed to say.

"That isn't what I heard. I heard you're the best in school."

"You did?"

"Are you the best in school?"

"I don't know," I stammered. "Maybe. I guess so."

"Well, I'm pretty good, too," she said. "I'll be at the roller rink tonight. Will you be there, Harold?"

Harold! She actually called me Harold. "I don't know. Maybe. I guess so."

"You'll be there," Kate Miller said, and she dropped my pencil back to the floor.

I was there, and, unfortunately, Billy was there with me. I had considered putting up a fight against his tagging along that night, but I didn't for fear that I wouldn't be allowed to go. At first, my parents were delighted that I was willing to take Billy with me without a fuss, but they finally decided it had something to do with my recent weirdness. I let it pass. Nothing could keep me from my appointment with Kate Miller: not rain, nor sleet, nor my neighbor.

"Listen, Billy," I said as we stepped away from Dad's station wagon at the skating rink. "Are you listening?"

"Sure," he answered, but I knew from experience that "sure" didn't necessarily mean the same thing to Billy that it did to me. More often than not, it meant maybe so, maybe not, and I was never sure when it meant what, or if it meant anything at all. This one time I wanted to be sure, but I would've settled for a maybe so.

"There's this girl that's kind of special, and I kind of want to skate with her tonight."

"I kind of want to skate with her tonight, too, Harold," Billy said.

"You can't even skate, Billy!" I said, raising my voice.

"Why are you mad with me, Harold?"

"I'm not mad at you," I said, taking a deep breath.

"Then will you teach me to skate, Harold?"

"I won't have much time to teach you tonight, Billy. Don't you remember? There's this girl that's kind of special. . . ."

"Then we'd better hurry up, since we don't have much time," Billy called over his shoulder as he ran to the rink ahead of me.

"One more thing, Billy," I shouted after him. "Let me know if you need to go to the bathroom. You won't forget, will you? You sometimes forget when you get excited. Let me know if you need to go, okay? Billy! Are you listening?"

"Sure," Billy replied in the distance.

I was relieved when I entered the rink. Kate was late, and I had some time to spend with Billy, some time to explain to him the importance of the night, some time to appease my parents by taking some time with Billy. I wasted none of the time. I put on my skates, tied Billy's laces, and helped him to the floor.

Billy was slow when it came to learning anything. Billy was slower when it came to learning to skate. I'd given him years of private lessons, but Billy had only mastered standing up on his skates. He could not move forward or backward, left or right. He could only stand on his skates, motionless for an hour at a time, content to watch me circle the rink, waving and shouting my name each time I passed, and bragging to everyone within the sound of his voice that his best friend, Harold, was the greatest skater in the whole world. "He's crazy about me," I told myself as my name echoed off the floor; but my smile faded as I thought with guilt that I didn't feel the same way about him.

I rubbed the seat of my pants several times in empathy for Billy that night. Billy took a dozen hard falls to the floor, but he kept bouncing back. He was like that. He wanted to learn to skate, to pump his arms, to lean with the turns. He kept bouncing back.

"Keep your ankles stiff, Billy," I instructed. "Skate on the little wheels, not on your ankles."

"Okay, Harold. I'll do it right this time." Down he went and up he came.

"Be careful!" I said. "I'm responsible for you tonight. If you kill yourself, my dad will kill me."

"Okay, I won't kill myself, Harold." Down he went and up he came.

"Hello, Harold," someone behind me said. I turned to greet Kate Miller, and I stared at her as though she was the most beautiful girl I had ever seen, which she was. "Can't you speak?" she asked.

"Hi, Kate," I said. It was the first time I had called

her by her name, and I felt that all barriers between us had suddenly crumbled.

"Aren't you going to say hello to me, Smith?" Renee Foster asked. She was standing by Kate, and I hadn't even noticed her. She and Kate had come to the rink together, and although I was happy to see Kate, I was less than pleased to see her companion.

I didn't like Renee Foster one little bit. She always used my last name when referring to me. Never Harold. Besides, she had beaten me to a pulp when we were in the third grade and had left me lying under the jungle gym with a bloody nose and a wounded ego that has not fully healed to this day.

"Hello, Foster," I responded.

"Who's your friend, Harold?" Kate asked, smiling at Billy.

"Uh, this is Billy," I answered. I always felt awkward when people first met Billy. "He's my next-door neighbor."

"I've never seen him at school," Kate said.

"Billy goes to another school," I explained.

I was going to leave it at that, but Billy went on, "I go to a special school 'cause I'm special, huh, Harold?"

"That's right, Billy." I spun around on my skates, trying to divert Kate's attention.

"Bull!" Renee Foster exclaimed, interrupting as usual. "Crazy Billy goes to a school for retards, and there's nothing special about it."

"I don't, do I, Harold?" Billy said, looking to me for reassurance.

"No, Billy, you don't," I said. "Renee is just teasing." I glared at her.

"Your buddy is a retarded reject and a pumpkin-headed numb brain," Renee said. She had a way with words. "Why else would everyone call him Crazy Billy?"

"Everybody don't call me Crazy Billy!"

"Your good buddy, Smith, calls you Crazy Billy," Renee said, smiling. She was getting back at me for hating her so much, and she was doing a good job of it.

My awkwardness turned into anger. Kate or no Kate, I couldn't allow Renee Foster to stand there telling Billy things she said I said, even if I *had* said them. My integrity was on the line, and I didn't want Billy to know how weak it was at times. "I think you'd better shut your mouth, Foster, before I shut it for you," I said.

"The last time you said that, Smith, you ended up flat on your back under a swing set."

"It was a jungle gym," I said. "But I'm bigger now, and if you don't shut your mouth, I'll flatten it as flat as your flat chest." I had hit a nerve, and Renee's eyes reflected it. She wanted breasts more than she wanted anything, even friends. I had compared her to Kate, and Renee had come up short. "Come on, Billy," I said, turning from an infuriated Renee Foster and a bewildered Kate Miller. "We don't need them. We can skate by ourselves."

"But I can't skate, Harold," Billy reminded me.

"Then we'll teach you, won't we, Harold?" Kate said as she skated to Billy's side, leaving Renee Foster all alone.

Kate was a better teacher than I. She was patient and fun. She laughed and talked with Billy as though he were a regular kid. Billy responded to Kate's kindness by showing an even greater desire to learn to skate. When it was time for Kate and me to skate by ourselves, Billy could be pushed straight ahead at an amazing speed. He usually fell after several feet, but twice he coasted to a standing stop. Billy beamed, and I thought he was going to start singing "Jesus Loves Me" at the top of his voice.

He didn't sing, but he kissed me full on the mouth instead: something he often did when he was exceptionally happy, something I often warned him not to do in the company of my friends. I had long since stopped giving explanations for Billy's actions, having learned that my embarrassment was explanation enough. Kate Miller read the explanation that was written across my purple face, and with a Kate Miller smile, she asked me to skate.

I was secretly relieved as we skated down the rink. Kate was a very good skater, but I was better. I enjoyed leading her around the rink, turning her, holding her. We even talked as we skated, and she made our conversation as easy as the skating. We talked about sports. We talked about the track team at school. Mostly we talked about me. It was a stimulating conversation.

"Thanks for being so nice to Billy," I said, changing the subject but hoping that Kate would bring us back to the main topic of discussion, which was me.

"Billy's a great kid," Kate said. "I wonder if he goes to the same school my little brother attends."

"Your little brother is retarded?" I asked, finding it hard to believe that the most beautiful girl at school could have a retarded brother. But it explained why she had taken to Billy so quickly.

"His name is Mike," she said.

"Mike is a neat name." I didn't know what else to say.

"Mike is a neat kid," Kate said. "He's my favorite kid in the world, and I think he'd still be my favorite even if he weren't my little brother."

I thought about Billy and wondered if I could ever say that about him.

"Billy's lucky," Kate said, surprising me. "He's a lot smarter than Mike."

"He is?" I'd never thought of Billy's being lucky or smarter than anyone.

"I wish Mike were as smart as Billy," Kate said. Her eyes focused on something in the distance. "I'm not sure if Mike knows who I am. He's nine years old and still wears diapers. He has to wear a foam rubber helmet because he hits his head a lot. Sometimes he does it on purpose."

"I'm sorry, Kate," I said, taking her hand.

"That's okay," she said, looking at me again. "I stopped

wondering about it a long time ago. It's just the way things are, that's all."

"I guess so," I said, feeling closer to Kate than ever. Mike and Billy had given us a common bond.

"I've heard that you're a better runner than you are a skater," Kate said, getting back to the main topic of discussion. "Is that true?"

"I don't know. Maybe. I guess so."

"Come on," said Kate. "Don't be so modest. You know you're a good runner, don't you?"

"Okay, I'm a good runner," I said, and Kate laughed.

I was having more fun than I'd ever had in my life as Kate and I skated around the rink holding hands. I was beaming, and the only thing that threatened my happiness was Billy. Each time Kate and I passed him, I heard him screaming with delight; but the screams had nothing to do with me. He even neglected to wave. Billy was preoccupied with Renee Foster, who was helping him learn to skate by pushing him across the floor near the rail, pushing him faster and faster each time Kate and I passed. Silently I questioned Renee's intentions, but everything was going too great to be spoiled by feelings of responsibility. I shrugged it off.

"If you're as good a runner as I think you are, I might watch one of your track meets," Kate said.

"Just one?"

"Maybe two. Maybe all of them. Do you think you're that good?"

"I don't know."

"Maybe?"

"I guess so."

Kate laughed. "You know so, Harold Smith," she said, dropping my hand and putting her arm around my waist.

I felt her fingers pressing against my side, her arm across my back, and I felt my head go dizzy, my feet go light. I wanted to leap into the night, but I stumbled instead of taking flight. I rocked from side to side with an out-of-control feeling I hadn't known since my first month on skates.

I lost my balance completely and crashed to the floor, bruising myself so severely that for the next several days I walked as though I had a cactus in my pants. On my first bounce, I saw Renee Foster vigorously pushing Billy across the rink in Kate's direction, and I finally realized what she was doing. She was using Billy to get at me, and there was nothing I could do about it.

"Push faster!" I heard Billy yell.

"Wait, Kate, don't skate!" I screamed as I bounced a second time. But Kate never heard my ridiculous rhyme. Her head was thrown back—she was laughing at my fall. She never saw Billy coming.

Billy saw Kate, but there was nothing he could do, since he didn't know how to do anything but skate in a straight line. Although he could bust it with the best of them, Billy had never practiced intentional falls. I watched helplessly as Kate and Billy came closer together. Renee

Foster finally released Billy, and then the inevitable happened.

It was terrible. Billy's hands hit Kate at chest level. I heard Kate's breath evacuate her lungs with a sudden, panicky gush; and then I heard the sound of tearing fabric. Kate fell backward onto the floor, and Billy fell on top of her. They flew at an amazing speed across the polished floor, a clump of arms and legs.

"Here they come, Smith," Renee Foster commented. "There they go, Smith."

"Help me, Harold!" Billy pleaded as they flew past.

"Get him off me, Harold!" Kate screamed, as she squirmed under Billy's death grip.

Smith, Smith, Harold, Harold. I was beginning to hate both names.

Renee Foster and I reached the two of them as they ricocheted off the side railing. I was awed by what I saw. Kate Miller was flat on her back, and her shirt was ripped open to the waist, exposing her bra. Billy straddled her, his hands still pressed against her breasts. "Let go of Kate, Billy," I said.

"Yes, let go of Kate, Crazy Billy," Renee Foster said.

"No, wait, Billy! Please don't move your hands yet," Kate Miller pleaded, trying to collect what was left of her shirt. "Please, Harold, turn around. Please don't look."

"Let go, Billy," I repeated without thinking. I couldn't move, I could only stare at the little I could see of Kate's chest.

"How's it feel, Billy?" Renee Foster asked. How could she be so cruel? I thought. And how come it was Billy and not me?

Kate was now trying frantically to push Billy away and cover herself at the same time.

"It feels squishy," Billy replied innocently, and he let go.

"That's because it's all *padding*, Billy," Renee sneered.

Renee's words didn't sink in until I looked more closely at Kate's chest, and then at her face, which had gone completely white.

"They're fake!" I blurted. Kate Miller's breasts, the subject of my last hundred dreams, were not breasts at all. She had a chest exactly like mine!

Suddenly I could move again, and I dragged Billy off of Kate. She tried to cover herself with her hands, although she could have used her thumbs. I looked away, and scolded Billy, "What have you done?"

"Billy poo-pooed, Harold," Billy answered.

And he had.

Now "poo-poo" might be an okay word for little kids and Billy to use, but I wasn't about to use it, especially in the mood I was in by the time Dad picked us up. I was mad at Billy, I was mad at Renee Foster, I was mad at myself; and Kate Miller was mad at all of us. She will probably hate me forever, I thought as I slammed the car door. I was not thinking straight when Dad asked how we'd enjoyed skating. Without hesitation, I informed the entire carload that Billy had poo-pooed in his pants, only I didn't say poo-poo. I used the vulgar instead. It was one of the three words my mother hated more than a dead rat in her meat loaf, and she wasn't pleased with me. No one was pleased with me, not even me. It had not been my day.

Chapter 3

It was not my day for the next several weeks. Kate Miller asked to be moved to another desk in science class on the following Monday, and I was left to sit next to Carol Crump, a hefty girl who fantasized about relationships and who kept dropping pencils in the aisle between us. Kate no longer wore her breasts to school, but she still had long chestnut hair, an olive complexion, dark eyes, and full lips. I was suddenly aware that my fetish was not Kate Miller's breasts. My obsession was Kate Miller herself.

"Kate," I called after her as we left science class the Monday following the Incident. She ignored me, and the distance between us grew with every step she took. I tried to keep pace with her, but the pain in my rear caused by my skating fall held me back. "Kate," I begged, as I entered the corridor.

"What do you want?" she asked finally, turning to face me twenty feet down the hall. The sharpness of her voice attracted the attention of the students mingling between classes, and they eavesdropped with shameless curiosity. I wanted it to be a private discussion between Kate and me, but each time I hobbled in her direction, she stepped back, creating an even greater distance between us. Finally, I gave into the fact that it was going to be a lengthy conversation.

"Are you mad at me?" I asked, realizing the stupidity of my question the very second it left my mouth.

"Mad at you, Harold? Me?" She was getting louder, and the number of eavesdroppers grew. "Why should I be mad at you? Unless, of course, it's because you're a low-life pervert, a real creep, a snake, a jerk, a leech, and a pumpkin-headed snot!" Kate certainly wasn't at a loss for words when she was angry.

"Can't we just forget Friday night and take it from here?" I asked.

"*Forget!*" said Kate, walking toward me at a quick pace. "Do you have any idea what you did?"

"I got you mixed up with Billy, and . . ." I sputtered, stumbling backward as Kate moved in for the kill. Our faces were less than a foot apart.

"Don't blame it on Billy, Harold Smith," Kate replied. She had suddenly begun to speak in a regular tone of voice, only the words came out crisp and overly enunciated; and strangely enough, her facial expression changed from one of anger to one of sadness. I didn't understand what was happening. "He had nothing to do with it. *You're* the one who took advantage of me."

"Me?" I'm sure my confusion didn't help things just then.

"Yes," Kate said. "You took the trust I had in you and stepped on it. You took the feeling I had for you and stepped on it. Don't you understand anything? It wasn't your body I wanted, Harold Smith. I cared for *you*. Had I wanted body, I would have gone after one that was at least a little more than average, Mr. Average Body.

"I cared for Harold Smith, but Harold Smith didn't care for me. You desired what you thought I had and nothing more. Well, I guess I fooled you. How's your desire now?" I saw that small tears had formed at the corners of her eyes before she turned and walked away.

"I love you, Kate Miller," I blurted to her retreating figure. Spontaneity can be both a vice and a virtue, depending on which side of the word one is standing.

"Stick it in your gym shorts," Kate replied without breaking stride. "And I hope you walk like that the rest of your unnatural life." When I turned to hobble to my next class, the girls in the corridor began to applaud and cheer Kate, while the boys jeered my inability to subdue the "weaker" sex. I just crawled under the nearest rock.

I was under a rock at home as well, my parents having grounded me for two weeks when I introduced them to my expanded vocabulary. My only outside companion during the prison term was Billy. On weekdays he was at my house ten minutes after the special education bus had deposited him on the front lawn. And on Saturdays, he was knocking on my door before Kate Miller's image had departed my waking dreams.

I got mad at Billy more easily than I got mad at anyone, and it wasn't until my less-than-pleasant talk with Kate that I realized Billy had been a victim at the skating rink and I had been a jerk. Although I knew I'd been wrong, apologizing for my anger was hard. But Billy had a way of taking the hard part and making it easier. He took the blame, which made my taking the blame not as hard to swallow.

"I'm sorry I got you in trouble, Harold," Billy said. "I didn't mean to fall on that girl or make you say that ugly word."

"It wasn't your fault. It was mine."

"I'm glad it was your fault, Harold."

"Want to play cards?" I asked, knowing his answer before he answered. Cards were a regular item with Billy and me.

"I sure do."

"What do you want to play?" I asked, knowing his answer before he answered. You really get to know a person when you serve time with him. Besides, Billy knew only one card game.

"I want to play Let's Go Fishing in the Big Blue Lake."

"It's just Go Fish, Billy."

"What's this card, Harold?" Billy asked, pointing to one of the cards lying faceup on the table. We always played Go Fish faceup.

"It's the king of hearts."

"The king of hearts, Harold?"

"You remember, Billy. A king is the boss of a whole country, and he lives in a castle that is surrounded by a moat."

"And the moat is full of alligators and snakes and lizards and porcupines, huh, Harold?"

"I'm not sure about the porcupines."

"Now I remember," Billy said and laughed as if I had tickled his feet. "That's what my mommy says I have."

"Your mother says that you have a porcupine?" I asked. Billy's remarks often confused me, but trying to understand them was an enjoyable challenge sometimes, especially when Go Fish played faceup was the only other game in town. The disturbing thing about finally understanding them was that they often seemed sensible to me, a fact I didn't feel like sharing with anyone.

"No, silly Harold," Billy said. "She don't say I have a porcupine."

"What does she say you have, Billy?"

"That," he said, pointing to the king of hearts.

"Your mother says you have a king?" I asked.

"Not a king, silly Harold," Billy said, and he placed his finger on the large red heart in the center of the card. "That. Mommy says I have that!" And Billy's mom was right. Billy had a great big king of hearts' heart.

Chapter 4

My grounding ended the day track season began, and I began to live each day for the after-school track practices. I loved running track for the same reason I loved roller skating: I was good at it.

I enjoyed team sports, too, but for a different reason. I liked the camaraderie of team sports more than the sports themselves. There were always new friends to be made each season whether you were a good player or bad, and, man, was I bad. I had played baseball every summer from the time I could hold a bat on my shoulders. I wasn't very good at it when I first started playing, and I never got any better. I had a real talent for dropping fly balls whenever they fell dead center into the pocket of my glove.

Track was different. My love for the sport started as early as elementary school when my class would play

Red Rover. How I loved that game. Unlike the baseball captains, the captains of Red Rover wanted to win the toss of the coin so they could choose me first. I was the fastest kid in the class—fast enough to break through the strongest of the Red Rover chains.

"Red Rover, Red Rover, send Harold right over." Sometimes I can still hear my classmates calling my name. Sometimes I can still see their faces wrinkle in anticipation as they tighten their grips on one another's hands, hold their breaths, and watch the master of the game ready himself for his run. Man, how I loved playing Red Rover, Red Rover, especially when it was my turn to come right on over.

But now that I was in junior high, I had decided to retire from Red Rover and concentrate my athletic energies on track. The 400-meter run was my chosen event: a race that went all the way around the track, a race that was less than ten yards shy of being a full quarter mile, a race that required both speed and stamina.

Since my Red Rover days it had been my dream to someday run in the Olympics, to represent my country in the greatest of world games. As a seventh-grader at Lakeside Junior High, the first step toward the Olympics was to earn a position on the ninth-grade varsity track team. It was rare for a seventh-grader to make the varsity, but over the years a few had achieved the honor. I wanted desperately to do the same, to take the first step on the road to the Olympics. Besides, I figured Kate Miller could not help but notice a seventh-grader who had made the ninth-grade varsity. I figured it was my only chance to win her back.

"Water break," Coach yelled midway through practice.

I was past ready for a water break. It was the third week of practice, and the coach had already increased our running assignments to the maximum. By the time he called for a break, everyone on the team was tired, thirsty, and had a bad case of cotton mouth—a white coating of dried saliva that grows on a runner's lips like mold and peels away like model airplane glue.

"Hello, Harold! Three guesses who's here, and the first two don't even count once." I looked up from the water fountain to see Billy running across the infield toward me, yelling at the top of his voice. Every afternoon when the special education bus deposited him at his house, Billy would check with his mom and head directly for Lakeside Junior High to watch me practice. "Did you guess it was me, Harold?"

"I guessed," I grumbled, aggravated that Billy always managed to step into my scenes whether I wanted him there or not.

"You win, you win," Billy said, clapping his hands in genuine exaltation.

"So give me a blue ribbon," I said, leaning over the fountain.

"Say, Goofy, are you waiting in line or are you trying to remember your name?" The question was directed at

Billy, and the person asking was Teddy Taylor. Teddy was one of those ninth-graders who condescended to everyone except those bigger than he. He lived three blocks down the street, and Billy and I had spent several summer afternoons avoiding him.

"My name ain't Goofy, and you know it," Billy replied.

"You calling me a liar, Goofy?" Teddy asked, smiling. Teddy always smiled when he was about to do something unfunny.

"Come on, Billy," I said, grabbing his arm and jerking him away from the water fountain. I was mad because he had put me in the middle again. "Let's walk over to the stands. You aren't supposed to be on the field."

"Not so fast, Smith," Teddy said, grabbing Billy's other arm. "Me and Goofy were having a friendly conversation."

"Why don't you just leave him alone?" I said as several runners gathered around the water fountain to gawk.

"Want to make me, Smith?" Teddy asked with a smile, having noticed the gathering himself.

"His name ain't Smith," Billy said. "His name is Harold. You must be dumber than me."

The crowd around the water fountain laughed at Billy's remark, and Teddy took it to mean that they were laughing at him. He held his smile, but his face steamed red.

"Don't call me dumb, Goofy," Teddy said, and he poked Billy's chest hard enough to cause him to stumble backward.

I made my decision. No one, not even Teddy Taylor,

was going to push Billy around and get away with it. Poking fun at Billy was one thing. Poking Billy was something else. I let go of Billy's arm, squared off with Teddy Taylor, and got ready to pop him in the mouth. I'd been whipped in the past. Renee Foster had done it in the third grade, so getting whipped by Teddy Taylor wouldn't be that big a deal.

"What's going on here?" The question came from behind me, and I turned to see Jake, the Snake, Blake approach the scene. Jake Blake was my hero at Lakeside. He was the best football player at school and the best wide receiver in the city. He got his nickname, Snake, because he was tall and skinny, and he could snatch a football out of midair about as quick as a snake could bite its prey. In addition to being the best football player at Lakeside, Jake was also the fastest 400-meter runner at school. When he was a seventh-grader, Jake had run one of the legs of the 1600-meter relay on the ninth-grade varsity. I had admired him from the first football game of the season, and he became my hero the first time I saw him run the 400-meter race during track practice.

Hero worship is nice as long as the hero is far enough away to obscure details. Before that day, I had always kept Jake at a distance. I had always been afraid to approach him, fearing that he might reject the friendship of a mere seventh-grader, and I have never been high on rejection.

But Jake violated the arrangement I had secretly made

with him when he walked onto the scene at the water fountain. My heart began to sink at the thought of losing a hero, and my face flushed with anger at the thought of Jake's joining forces with his ninth-grade cohort. I had already made my decision concerning Teddy Taylor, and it could be expanded to include Jake Blake.

"What's going on here?" Jake asked again. He was six inches taller than anyone on the track team and usually didn't have to ask questions twice.

"This boy is pushing me around, mister," Billy said.

Jake Blake stepped between Teddy Taylor and me and looked down into Teddy's face. "Coach wants to see you, Teddy," Jake said.

"In a minute, Jake," Teddy said. "I've got some unfinished business here."

"Coach wants to see you right now, Taylor," Jake said, and the crowd around us gasped. Jake had called Teddy by his last name—something a ninth-grader never did to a fellow ninth-grader at Lakeside. It did not make Teddy happy, and he dropped his smile. There's tough and there's tough, and Teddy Taylor knew the difference as he walked away from the water fountain, cotton mouth still stuck to his lips.

Jake Blake turned to me. "Coach wants to see you, too, Smith," he said.

"His name ain't Smith, mister," Billy said. "His name is Harold."

"Okay," Jake said with a grin. "Coach wants to see you, Harold." The crowd around us let out another little gasp. Ninth-graders never called seventh-graders by their first names at Lakeside.

"Coach wants me?" I asked.

"Right now," Jake said.

"Billy, I want you to sit in the stands and stay there until I come to get you after practice," I said. "You can see everything from the stands, so stay there. Okay, Billy?"

"Okay, Harold."

"I appreciate the way you treated Billy," I told Jake as the two of us walked toward the track. "Some of the guys give him a hard time."

"A kid's a kid," Jake said, and I realized that some people are born to be heroes.

"What does Coach Barksley want with me?" I asked.

"He wants you to run 400 meters with me."

"What? With you?"

"Coach hasn't found the fourth person for the 1600-meter relay, and it looks like he has his eye on you," said Jake.

"I have a chance to make the varsity?"

"I imagine it depends on how well you run this race," Jake said. "The Lakeside Relays are only six weeks away, so Coach needs to know who has a chance."

The Lakeside Relays was the first track meet of the season. It was also one of the biggest meets of the year; but more importantly, Lakeside Junior High was the host school, and my peers would be looking on from the stands. Kate Miller would be looking on from the stands. There would be ten schools participating in the meet—almost four hundred track shoes—and out of all those track shoes, I thought that maybe, just maybe, Kate Miller would be looking at only one pair.

As Jake and I neared the track, my thoughts were interrupted by a swarm of butterflies that had suddenly set up housekeeping inside my stomach. The little monsters took complete control of my nerves that afternoon. I was as sick to my stomach as I had been the day I ate ten tablespoons of mayonnaise on a dare, and I felt as though any minute I was going to drop dead. I knew it, and I wanted it.

"You'd better start warming up for the race," said Jake. "We're going to run any minute now."

"Okay, Jake, I'll try," I said.

"You don't look so good. Are you feeling okay?"

"I feel terrible," I answered honestly. How could I lie when I was about to taste the end of my life? "I'm sick."

"You going to vomit?"

The word made my stomach churn. "Maybe," I answered.

"It's just the butterflies. We all get them. They'll go away as soon as the race begins."

"Honest?" There was hope.

"Most of the time," Jake said.

"Most of the time? Oh, no, I'm really going to be sick."

"If you're going to be sick, you'd better visit the old oak tree," Jake said.

"The what?"

"The old oak tree. You know, the one near the 300-meter mark on the outside of the track. It's where everybody goes to throw up the butterflies. It's tradition here at Lakeside."

"Are you serious?"

"Sure, I'm serious," Jake said, "but you'd better hurry. There's not much time left for throwing up. That's a luxury at track practice, you know."

"I'll try to hurry."

I hadn't taken three steps when a dreadful announcement came from Coach Barksley. "I'm ready for Blake and Smith to run," he said. The words resounded across the infield. I wobbled a little faster toward the oak tree and deliverance.

"Wait a minute, Harold," Jake said, running to stop me. "It's too late for the oak tree. Coach wants us now."

"No, Jake, I can't do it. I can't run the race. I can hardly walk."

"Come on," Jake commanded, grabbing my arm. "You're a seventh-grader running with a ninth-grader. You've got to prove yourself."

"I can't do it, Jake," I said, jerking free of his grasp. "I'm going to be sick. I know I am."

"Okay," Jake said, patting my shoulder. "Don't worry about it."

"Thanks."

"Think nothing of it, Smith."

Jake turned and jogged toward the starting line for the 400-meter run, and I turned toward the old oak tree and defeat. My stomach was churning worse than ever, and a sour, acid taste backed into my throat. I felt terrible, but I felt even worse about missing my chance to make the varsity.

"I see you, Harold," a voice called suddenly from the stands. "Do you see me over here, Harold?" It was Billy. He was standing at the bottom of the stadium, behind the gate that separated the runners from the fans.

Billy was waving to me, his hands high over his head. His shirttail had slipped out of his pants and had crawled up his waist. It was a ridiculous sight: Billy, with his round stomach exposed, waving his arms, and wearing a dumb-looking smile that invited everyone in town to take a cheap shot at it.

"Hi, Billy," I managed to say.

"I'm going to watch you race," Billy screamed. "Three cheers for my friend Harold. Yea, Harold. Yea, Harold. Yea, Harold." It was a ridiculous, embarrassing, inspiring sight. I turned from the old oak tree and moved slowly toward the starting line to run against Jake Blake.

"I knew you'd give it a try," Jake said as I stepped onto the cinders of the track. "I'm in lane one, and you're in lane two."

"Thanks," I managed to mumble, trying not to open my mouth.

"Runners, take your marks!" Coach Barksley commanded.

"Good luck," said Jake, behind me in lane one. I

nodded my head as I backed into the starting blocks.

"Get set!" Coach snapped, and my rear rose slowly into the air.

"BAM!" sounded the starter's gun.

And we were off!

I had come out of the blocks to the sound of the gun so often in practice that it had become a conditioned reflex, and I jolted from the starting blocks without thinking about my stomach. By the time I reached the 100-meter mark, my stomach had settled a little, and I began to concentrate more on the race and less on my butterflies.

As I came out of the first curve into the backstretch, I could hear Jake's footsteps behind me. I did not have any idea how far back he was, and I knew better than to look.

I paced myself on the back straightaway, and I felt good going into the far curve. I even began to think about winning as I approached the 300-meter mark.

The old oak tree on the outside of the track loomed ahead of me. Its buckled branches hung over the edge of the cinders like the heads of sick runners from years past. It seemed to beckon to me.

"You're coming into my lane," Jake shouted as I veered to the left away from the tree. My stomach churned, and I slowed my pace. Jake was almost to my side when I stumbled in front of him, and my stomach finally heaved as we collided and fell to the cinders. What an embarrassment. What a mess. It happened in front of the whole track team, and I knew it was all over for me, the seventh-grade wonder boy.

"I'm sorry, Jake," I heard myself say.

"Get up, Harold," Jake said. "We've got to finish this race."

"But I'm still sick," I whined. "Besides, I've already lost."

"That doesn't matter," said Jake, pulling me to my knees. "What really matters is finishing."

"I'll try," I said, getting to my feet.

"Hold my hand and I'll help you finish," Jake said. "Yuck! Wipe that stuff onto the seat of your shorts first. That's it. Now, give me your hand again."

Jake and I jogged toward the finish line. I felt ridiculous holding his hand in front of the entire track team, but I would have fallen without his support. I was humiliated enough without crumbling to the cinders again.

As Jake and I approached the finish line, our teammates erupted in mock cheers. They laughed, they whistled, they blew us kisses. My head slumped to my chest.

"Think pleasant thoughts," Jake said. "In twenty years some of them won't even remember this."

"Somehow that doesn't make me feel any better."

Suddenly, I heard a voice bellowing over all the others. "That's my friend Harold!" the voice yelled. "Run faster, Harold. You can beat that boy. Yea, Harold. Yea, Harold. Yea, Harold." At the sound of Billy's cheers, I lifted my head, lengthened my stride, and crossed the finish line a half step ahead of Jake.

Coach Barksley wasn't angry, which surprised me. In fact he was very nice. It was as if he had seen the same thing happen before, or maybe it had even happened to him. Anyway, he knelt downwind from me and offered some good advice. "Try never to vomit while you're running a race," he said. "And in four weeks make sure you're in the best shape of your life. The Lakeside Relays are in six weeks, and I need to know who's going to run the 1600-meter relay two weeks before that."

"You're giving me another chance, Coach?"

"You finished the race," he said, moving a little to the right as the wind shifted. "You deserve another chance. Now hit the showers before you make everyone else sick."

Before I threw up all over myself, I had always been totally embarrassed whenever I had to take a shower with thirty other guys after track practice. Standing naked in a room full of naked boys getting ready to shower away the odor of exercise was not my idea of a good time, especially since I was a little taller than small and still waiting for puberty to jump on my body.

However, I was too embarrassed about what had happened to feel embarrassed about anything else. Not even the ninth-graders embarrassed me as they sauntered into the shower with their extra two years of maturity dangling before them. I lay on my back on the tiled floor while the steaming water splashed and revitalized my aching body, and I tried to think about the good news. I had been given a second chance.

Chapter 5

So much for the good news. The bad news was that the following day I had to go to school, where I became the object of some very humiliating and not-so-funny jokes.

"Whose initials are B.B.S.?" one joke began. "Barf Bag Smith" was the answer. There were others. "What goes with regurgitated fish?" Answer: "Harold Smith's jockstrap." Still others. "If Harold Smith swallowed a navy bean, a lima bean, and a green bean, how many beans would be in his stomach?" Answer: "None for very long." And more. "How is Lakeside's track team different from other track teams?" Answer: "Lakeside runners hold hands instead of batons." That particular joke did not last long on the Lakeside joke circuit because Jake Blake didn't find it amusing, and the boy who authored the joke went home that afternoon with the imprint of the bottom of Jake's jogging shoe across his rear end.

I stalked Kate Miller the day of my humiliation. I wanted to know where she was every minute of the day because I didn't want her to know where I was any minute of the day. I tolerated everyone else's jokes, but I could not have tolerated a joke from Kate. I had to avoid her at all costs. I was afraid of a chance meeting with Kate, and I decided to give the chance meeting no chance by keeping chance out of it.

I watched Kate every possible minute at school that day. I was careful not to let her see me lurking in the shadows of the hall, peeking around corners, looking over the shoulders of other students. I gulped my lunch down in half the time it normally took me to eat and hurried out the back door of the cafeteria because I knew that on sunny days Kate always left by the front.

"What are you doing, Harold Smith?" Kate asked, and I cleared the ground at the sound of her voice.

"What?" I asked, after a quick landing. Kate had sneaked up behind me.

"What are you doing?" she asked again.

"I'm just standing here. Any law against that?"

"What have you been doing all day?" Kate asked.

"What do you mean?"

"You know exactly what I mean," she said. "Every time I've turned around today, you've been watching me, lurking in the shadows of the hall, peeking around corners, looking over the shoulders of other students.

Tell me something, Harold. How many times have I gone to the girls' room today?"

"How should I know?"

"You shouldn't know, but you do," Kate said. "How many times?"

"I don't keep track of your rest room trips," I lied.

"How many times, Harold?"

"Twice," I said quietly.

"I bet you even remember the times."

"Nine thirty and eleven forty-five," I said, again very quietly.

"Do you want to tell me why you've been following me, Harold?"

"No."

"Are you this weird around everyone, Harold?"

"No."

"Is there something you want to tell me, Harold?"

"No."

"No?"

"Yes."

"Yes no, or yes yes?"

"Yes yes, I guess."

"Then go ahead and tell me," Kate said. "I wouldn't miss this for anything."

"Do you know any good jokes?" I asked, giving her the opportunity to humiliate me just as I had humiliated her at the skating rink.

"Are we in the same world, Harold?"

"What?"

"I don't have any idea what you're talking about," Kate said. "You act weird all morning and now you want me to tell you a joke. One of us is in another place and time."

"You haven't heard what happened to me yesterday at track practice?" I asked. "You haven't heard the jokes going around school today?"

"Oh, those jokes," Kate said.

"Those jokes."

"Why would I want to tell you one of those jokes? Haven't you heard enough of them?"

"I thought you might like to get even."

"I need to tell you something, Harold," Kate said, stepping closer to me. "I've thought a lot about what happened at the skating rink, and I've decided that if the tables were turned and you were lying naked on the skating rink floor instead of me, I would have done to you what you did to me."

"You're kidding!"

"Afraid not," Kate said, smiling, and I saw a side of Kate I had never seen. A racy side. I thought about it a minute and decided that all girls should have a racy side. Except mothers, of course.

"I need to tell you something, too, Kate," I said. "I've thought about it, and I've decided that you're the prettiest girl in school, with or without breasts; and if your breasts never grew for the rest of your life, I'd still think you were the prettiest girl around."

"Thanks," Kate said. "I think."

"You're welcome."

"Now that we've settled that," Kate said, "how would you and Billy like to come over to my house Saturday night?"

"Are you serious?"

"Of course I'm serious," Kate said. "I've been trying to ask you all day, but every time I came near you, you vanished into the crowd or crawled under a water fountain. I was beginning to wonder if you were still crazy about me."

"I'd love to come," I said, ignoring her remark.

"What about Billy? Do you think he'd like to come, too?"

"Anything I like to do, Billy likes to do, too."

"Good," Kate said. "I want the two of you to meet my brother, Mike. He hasn't been able to go to his school for a couple of weeks because he hasn't been feeling well. In fact, we've been worried about him. I thought some friends and fireworks might cheer him up."

"Fireworks?"

"We saved some from New Year's Day," said Kate. "Mike loves fireworks."

"So does Billy."

"Good," she said. "Saturday night?"

"Saturday night," I said, and Kate turned to walk away.

"Kate?" I called after her.

"Yes?"

"I am," I said.

"You're what?"

"Still crazy about you."

"I know," she said and walked away.

Chapter 6

When I awoke Saturday morning, the sun was beginning to lap at the corners of my drapes, and Billy was tapping on my window. "Are you awake, Harold?" Billy asked from outside my window, his fingers still tapping against the glass. Tap, tap, tap. Tap, tap, tap. I pulled my pillow from under my stomach and covered my face with it. Billy was persistent. Tap, tap, tap. Tap, tap, tap. "Are you awake, Harold?"

"No," I said, pushing the pillow from my face and sitting on the edge of my bed.

"You look like you're awake, Harold."

"Okay, I'm awake," I said, focusing on my watch, which lay on my bedside table. "Geez, Billy. It's only seven o'clock in the morning, and it's Saturday morning."

"I know, Harold," said Billy, his mouth pressed against my window. "What do you want to do today?" he mumbled into the glass, fogging the pane with his breath.

"I want to go back to sleep," I said, falling back into bed.

Tap, tap, tap. Tap, tap, tap.

"Okay, okay, I'm getting up," I said. "Don't stick your tongue on the window, Billy. Birds mess on windows."

"Yuck," Billy said, spitting several times before pulling his tongue back into his mouth.

"What are you doing here, anyway?"

"Waiting for you. Want to play Let's Go Fish in the Lake today?"

"I'm going to work out at the track this morning, Billy."

"How about this afternoon?"

"I'm going to work out at the track this afternoon, too," I said. "As a matter of fact, I'm going to work out every Saturday morning and afternoon, and I'm going to work out every weekday afternoon after I work out with the track team. I'm going to make the ninth-grade varsity as a seventh-grader. Whatever it takes, I'm going to do it."

"Good, Harold," Billy said, "but I gotta get dressed first."

"What?"

"I gotta get dressed first."

"You aren't dressed?"

"I got on my pajamas, Harold. It's only seven o'clock in the morning, you know. I gotta get dressed so I can go run track with you."

"You aren't going to run track with me," I said. "Not now, not ever." I could afford to be blunt because I knew my parents would back me on this one. They knew how important track was to me. They knew it was an individual sport that took concentration, and they knew I couldn't look after Billy while I was running.

"Why can't I run track with you, Harold?" Billy asked. He had already stripped down to his underwear in order to save some time dressing at his house.

"You might get hurt," I said.

"I won't get hurt, Harold."

"Put your pajamas back on, Billy. I don't want you to go, and that's that."

I left my house alone that morning and rode my bicycle to the Lakeside track. I began what was to become a six-day-a-week training program that would continue for the next four weeks, until Coach Barksley would give me a second chance to make the ninth-grade varsity.

The track was different on Saturday morning. I had never seen it when it wasn't alive with runners setting their blocks, running sprints, and exchanging batons. I stood on the cinders and surveyed the oval track. There was no one there to laugh if I fell, no one there to jeer if I got sick. I felt good being there.

I stretched my leg muscles and completed the routine warm-up exercises. After the warm-up exercises, I ran several sprints down the track, concentrating on my speed. When I was satisfied with my speed, I set the starting blocks and got ready to run my first 400 meters of the day.

There were no sounds on the track to break my concentration as I backed into the starting blocks. I took several deep breaths, raised my rear, and shot out of the blocks. I sprinted to the 100-meter mark, then paced myself along the backstretch. I loved the feel of the breeze that my speed created and the crunching sound my feet made on the cinders. I reached the 300-meter mark, and I made my move without glancing at the oak tree at the side of the track. I sprinted the last 100 meters and crossed the finish line winded and tired, but I was still on my feet and my breakfast was still in my stomach.

"Yea, Harold! Yea, Harold! Yea, Harold!" The words came from high in the stands, and without looking up, I knew who had yelled them. Billy.

"What are you doing here?"

"I came to watch you, Harold."

"Don't you have anything better to do?" I yelled.

"Nope."

"Well, find something better to do."

"Why, Harold?"

"Because I don't want you here!" I screamed. "Go home!"

It took five full seconds for my scream to settle over the track, and it took less than five seconds for Billy to start to cry. I couldn't see the tears because he was up in the stands, but I knew he was crying. His shoulders slumped, his hands fell to his sides, and he turned his face from me. He was crying, no doubt about it.

Billy didn't cry very often, because he knew I hated

it, and I hated it because I was usually the cause of it. I hated it so much that I sometimes apologized.

"I'm sorry," I yelled to Billy, who was making his way down the stands. When he got to the bottom and started walking away, I kind of apologized again. "I said I was sorry. What else do you want?"

"You mean it, Harold?" Billy asked as he turned toward me.

"I said it, didn't I?"

"Yes," Billy answered, and he stood there wiping his eyes, wondering what to do.

"Come on," I said, motioning for him to follow me. "You can watch from the side of the track."

"Really, Harold?"

"I said so, didn't I? But you can't get on the track. Got it, Billy?"

"I got it, Harold," Billy answered, and he patted me on the back. "Is it okay if I tell you to take your mark, get set, and go when you race?"

"I guess it's okay," I said, backing into the starting blocks.

"Runners, take your marks, Harold," Billy said. "Get set, Harold. Go, Harold! Go. Go. Go. Go. Go."

I rode my bicycle home from the track after my Saturday-morning workout while Billy jogged beside me. Billy had a bicycle exactly like mine and could ride it almost as well as I could ride mine, as long as his training wheels were attached and he stayed on the sidewalk and the wind was not blowing too hard; but he was not allowed to venture off our block riding it, not even with me.

That afternoon I let Billy tag along beside me to the Lakeside track for the second half of my weekend practice. He thanked me at least a dozen times for letting him come, and he told me what a great runner I was at least a dozen more. I decided then and there that Billy could attend all my secret practice sessions. I knew he would show up at the track anyway, and besides, flattery works on me like sunshine after a rain. I figured I was due some warm praise.

Billy stood on the infield at the edge of the track and watched me exercise. When I completed my warm-up drills, I shed my sweatpants and exchanged my jogging shoes for my track cleats. I noticed that Billy was especially interested in my track shoes, with their special cleats for running on cinders.

"Ice pick shoes," he said, staring down at them.

"Track shoes," I corrected. "They help with traction and speed on the cinders."

"Track shoes," Billy said, "with little ice picks on the bottoms."

After completing my sprints, I took some time to teach Billy how to use the starting blocks. I'd learned that spending a little time with him could save a lot of time in questions. I showed him how to back into the blocks, how to place his hands on the track, how to lift his rear in the air on the get set signal, and how to come out of the blocks low, gradually raising his body in order to attain the most speed from the start.

Billy loved it, and he was much better than I had expected he would be, even though his right leg made it difficult for him to run any distance without stumbling or falling to the cinders. Since the day we fell from the tire swing, Billy had raised his right leg much higher than his left when he ran.

As I watched him come out of the starting blocks and run his fifty-yard sprints, I wondered how good a runner he might have been had he not tripped in the tire swing: had we not tripped: had I not tripped. Except for his right foot, which flew higher into the air than his left foot did—causing him to sway, then compensate, then sway, then fall—Billy had the right stuff to be a good runner. He had great endurance; he had good speed; he had a natural start; and more important than anything else, Billy had heart.

"Get your rear a little higher," I said as Billy readied himself for the gun. "That's it. Now, don't forget to come out low, and try not to stumble so soon this time."

"Okay, Harold. I'll try."

"BAM!" I said, and Billy was off. He swerved into lane two, back into lane one, back into lane two. At the forty-yard mark he stumbled, but he righted himself before he hit the cinders. He finished the fifty-yard sprint in lane three, but he finished on his feet, and I could see his smile fifty yards down the track.

I ran my remaining 400-meter runs that day while Billy watched from the infield, urging me on to victory. Billy jumped up and down, screaming his head off for me to win, and since I was the only runner on the track, I didn't disappoint him.

"You won again, Harold," Billy said after my final race of the day.

"I was the only one running, Billy."

"That's right, and you came in first," Billy said. It was no wonder that my ego was more inflated than other egos my age.

Billy and I laughed most of the way home from practice that afternoon. I was going to see Kate Miller at her house that night, and the thought warmed my insides. Billy was going to Kate's house, too, but he was smiling because he had worked out on the track with me. We felt great, and as we walked home, Billy sang "Jesus Loves Me" allegro, swinging his hips to the tune, and clapping his hands.

Chapter 7

Since I was a little kid, I have known that good feelings do not last forever. One day it's Red Rover, Red Rover, send Harold right over. But the next day it's baseball instead of Red Rover, and everyone knows I'm a right-field substitute, the designated hitter's designee. The feeling of euphoria has vanished completely.

Euphoria is a good word. Billy and I were filled with it as we walked to Kate's house that Saturday night. We stepped lightly, thinking of fireworks and celebration and friends. Billy sang two of his favorite songs, which he had somehow merged into one. As he sang, I listened, and the sky was flecked with white, puffy animal-cracker clouds that seemed to float within arm's reach.

"Come on in, guys," Kate said as she greeted us at the door. "The fireworks will start as soon as it's dark."

"Oh, boy, I love firecrackers," Billy said. "But I'm not supposed to pop them unless Harold helps me. Did you know that Harold tongue kisses wart frogs?"

"What?" Kate asked, and she cast a furtive glance in my direction.

"One time I popped a firecracker in my hand," Billy said. "Right here. See? It made a black bubble, and Harold stuck it with a pin, and it hurt real bad, and blood gushed out, and Harold wouldn't kiss it and make it better. Harold said he'd rather tongue kiss a wart frog than kiss my bloody hand and make it all better."

Kate saw my red face and came to my rescue. "We won't embarrass you tonight, Harold, will we, Billy?" she said. "Tonight everyone is going to have a good time because tonight is special."

"Why is it special?" Billy asked.

"Because my two favorite friends and my favorite and only brother are here," Kate said. "Come on, fellows. Mike and my parents are in the backyard."

Kate introduced us to her parents. I looked around the yard for Kate's little brother, Mike, but all I saw was the back of a little kid's wheelchair. The chair was much too small for a nine-year-old. I decided that Mike was still inside the house.

"Follow me, boys," Kate said to Billy and me. "I want to introduce you to the greatest kid on the block."

Kate led us straight to the empty little wheelchair in the yard, only it was not empty. When Kate turned it around, we saw Mike for the first time. He was the smallest nine-year-old I had ever seen. Mrs. Damico, the meanest lady on my block, had a five-year-old brat of a grandson who was larger than Mike. The little boy was tied in his chair with a cloth belt. He was wearing a helmet that was made of foam rubber or something, and it came down to his ears and wrapped all the way around his head. "Mike hasn't been feeling well," Kate told us, and she turned to her brother. "How are you, sport?" Kate asked, but Mike stared straight ahead and did not answer.

"Why don't he say something?" Billy asked.

"Mike can't say anything," Kate replied as she tried unsuccessfully to brush down a tuft of hair that stuck out from underneath little Mike's foam helmet.

"He can't talk?" I asked incredulously and wished immediately that I could take back the question.

"No, Mike can't say a word," Kate said.

"Then what's he good for?" Billy asked, and I wanted to stuff a wart frog down his throat.

"He's good for me," Kate said, "just like you are good for Harold."

"Huh?"

"It's hard to explain," Kate said, "but Harold understands." Kate was right. I did understand. "He needs some sun," Kate continued. "That's the one thing about the special school I don't like. They don't get him outside enough."

"They get him outside, Kate," Mrs. Miller said from the patio.

"It doesn't look like it," Kate replied. "I've never seen him with a tan."

Mike's skin was as pale as the faded rubber duck that Billy had bathed with since he was a baby. Mike's coal black hair was a stark contrast to his skin, and it stuck out in all directions from having been groomed by foam rubber helmets all his life. His arms and legs were small, even in relation to the rest of his body, and his veins were as blue against his skin as his hair was black against his forehead. His lips met to form neither a smile nor a frown. Even his eyes showed no expression. They were large and dark, and they seemed to stare past all of us to another place where only he was allowed to visit.

For no apparent reason, Mike's head suddenly slumped to one side and rested wearily on his shoulder. In the dim light of the evening, I noticed that a piece of the foam helmet had been cut away. I saw what appeared to be a bald spot the size of my fist behind little Mike's ear; and where a patch of hair once grew, there were only scars and a mass of deep, purple bruises. In the center of the deepest, most recent wound was a small red spot about the size of a dime where the blood had found its way close to the surface of Mike's abused head.

"Mike hits his head against things," Kate said, having seen that I had noticed her brother's very noticeable wound.

"Why?"

"No one knows why. He just does. That's why he wears the foam helmet. But sometimes it doesn't help. We cut away the foam around the sore so the pressure wouldn't hurt him all the time, and soon, he'll be as good as new. Soon, you'll be as good as new," Kate repeated to Mike.

Mike didn't seem to have heard what she said. With one small hand, he covered his eyes, and with his other hand, he quickly slapped the sore at the back of his ear. Then little Michael Miller screamed as if he were being tortured by Beelzebub himself.

"Moaieeeeeeeeee!" he screamed. "Moaieeeeeeeeee!" It shattered the calmness in Kate's backyard like an unfamiliar noise in the night shatters sleep. His dark eyes darted to the right and left, up and down in search of an escape from the reality of pain back to that peaceful place where only he was admitted.

The Millers jumped into action at the sound of Mike's cry. Kate held Mike's arms while Mr. Miller cradled Mike's head with his hands. Mrs. Miller ran inside and then back outside with a warm compress in one hand and a bandage in the other. Billy and I stood at a distance and watched until Mrs. Miller pressed the warm cloth on Mike's erupted sore. When he screamed again, I turned from the scene and wished I could go home. "The worst part is over, Mike," I heard Kate say. "The worst part is over," she said again. I looked at Kate and saw that she, too, was unable to look upon her younger brother's torment. Her hands held Mike's hands, but her eyes were turned away from the dark, haunting eyes of the little boy in the wheelchair. His eyes were filled with pain, and Kate's eyes were filled with a different kind of pain. "The worst part is over, Mike," Kate said again, and as she leaned over and kissed her brother's wound to make it all better, I fell in love with her all over again.

Billy had not made a sound during the entire ordeal, and I looked at him to make sure he was okay. I was surprised to see him watching Mike, staring at him. The moon pushed away the evening clouds, and I saw that the boy with the king of hearts' heart was crying.

"Look at something else, Billy," I whispered, but he didn't hear me.

Mike's screams eased to a whimper. Then he was quiet. Once again he stared silently, and his dark eyes seemed to penetrate the darkness.

"He's okay now," Kate said. "Come over here for a minute, and then we'll start the fireworks."

"Okay, Kate," I said, as I grabbed Billy's arm and pulled him cautiously over to where Kate kneeled beside Mike's wheelchair. I was on my guard, just in case Mike decided to hurt himself again.

"Watch what Mike does," Kate said, and Billy and I knelt beside the wheelchair. Kate began to stroke Mike's face with the backs of her hands. Over and over again, her hands caressed her brother's pale cheeks. Just as I was beginning to wonder what it was that Mike was supposed to do, a smile appeared on his small face. Kate continued to rub with her fingers, and the boy's face glowed like the moon against the backdrop of the night. Billy leaned over and whispered something in his ear, and Mike Miller gazed into the night and past the darkness.

Dad picked us up at Kate's house after the last of the fireworks had streaked the heavens. Billy and I sat in the backseat of the station wagon in silence on the way home, leaving behind the fading odor of burning Roman candles and celebration. Our silence must have disturbed Dad because his mirrored eyes kept looking back at us. "Is everything okay, boys?" he asked as he pulled the station wagon into the garage. "Anything I can do to put smiles on those gloomy faces?"

"Everything's okay, Dad," I said, opening the back door. "I'm going to walk Billy home."

Billy grabbed me by the arm. "Stay with me for a little while, Harold," he whispered.

"Is it okay if Billy and I sit on his front porch for a little while, Dad?"

"Only if it will cheer both of you up," Dad said, messing our hair as he guided us out of the garage.

I have always loved Billy's front porch. It was longer than ours, and deeper. A kid could get a good running start and jump almost to the oak tree that shaded the entire front yard. The gray wooden floor was at least two feet off the ground, and anyone could be heard walking across it at night, even Dracula. On one end of the porch was a swing that was large enough for four and a half kids, and it creaked under the burden of its passengers.

I can remember Billy and me sitting in our moms' laps in that swing, falling asleep to the swing's steady creaking and to our moms' steady chatter.

"Billy, is that you?" Billy's mom asked from inside the house as we walked across the noisy porch to the swing.

"It's me and Harold, Mommy," answered Billy. "We're going to swing."

"Don't swing too high," his mom said.

Billy and I settled in the swing. We pushed with our feet to set it in motion, our knees straightening in front of the swing and then doubling under it while our feet remained in place on the floor of the porch. We hadn't swung together for ages, but that night it felt good, sitting quietly and listening to the summer night's concert. The crickets rubbed their musical legs together, and the swing's chains creaked against the beam near the ceiling. The wind whistled down the long porch and rustled the leaves of the oak tree in the front yard. It was one of those nights a boy is destined to recall on some warm summer evening in his manhood; and his reminiscence will make him happy, and his reminiscence will make him sad.

"Do you know what I whispered to that little boy, Harold?" Billy asked, hushing the legged section of the orchestra.

"No, Billy, I don't."

"It's kind of a secret, Harold."

"I understand. You don't have to tell me."

"Thanks, Harold."

"You're welcome," I said, and we sat without talking

long enough for the crickets to begin tuning their instruments before Billy broke our silence again.

"Will I ever be like that little boy, Harold?" Billy asked.

"No, never," I answered.

"I won't never be like you, neither, will I, Harold?"

"No, never," I answered.

"Something to think about, huh?"

"Something to think about."

"Something not to think about, too, huh, Harold?"

"Something not to think about, too," I answered.

"I whispered that I loved him, Harold," Billy said, and I placed my arm around his shoulder as the crickets harmonized with the leaves and the branches and the swing and the wind.

Chapter 8

It was too quiet in my room that night, and I didn't sleep well. I tossed and turned and went to the bathroom at least a hundred times. I heard Mom's mantel clock strike twelve as I settled into bed. When I finally closed my eyes, I dreamed about something that happened when Billy and I were nine years old.

It was Christmas, the year that Santa gave Billy his bicycle—the one that was exactly like mine. We were riding down the sidewalk, he was lagging far behind. "Hurry up, Billy," I yelled to him, and he pedaled with all the speed he could muster. "Hurry up!" I yelled again, and I looked back in time to see him lose control of his bicycle and veer into the street. I saw the approaching car, but there was nothing I could do except hold my breath and whisper "Please, God" a couple of times.

Brakes squealed, and Billy and his new bicycle fell to

the pavement. It looked as though the automobile had knocked Billy to the street, and I sped to the scene of the accident, hoping, praying that Billy was okay, but knowing in my heart that he was dead.

Luckily for Billy, my heart does not know all it pretends to know. I jumped off my bicycle and ran over to him. He was lying on his back, looking up at me. I scanned the immediate area for pools of blood, but there were none. There was not even a drop of blood on the street, and Billy's bicycle was not bent or scratched.

"Is he okay?" the driver of the car asked.

"Are you okay?" I asked.

"I'm okay, Harold," Billy answered.

"He's okay."

"He's okay?"

"He's okay, okay?"

"Okay."

I helped Billy to his feet and together we pushed his bicycle to the sidewalk. The driver opened his car door, but before he got inside, he turned to Billy and me once again. I knew exactly what he was going to say. "He's okay, mister," I said, hoping he would let it alone.

"Fine," the driver said, letting it alone. He got in his car and drove away slowly.

"Damn you, Billy," I said after the car had pulled away.

"Ooh, Harold, you said a dirty word," Billy said. "Ooh, your daddy's gonna get you good."

"I ought to get you good."

"Why do you want to get me good?"

"You almost got yourself killed!"

"I'm sorry I almost got myself killed, Harold. I won't do it no more. Honest."

"You'd better not. I mean it. I won't let you ride your bike anymore if you do that again."

"If I do what again, Harold?"

"If you ride too fast," I answered.

"But do you remember that you told me to hurry up and that's why I was riding so fast and that's why I almost got myself run over and that I wouldn't have done it if you had slowed down for me?"

I remembered. "I remember," I said. "That was a stupid thing for me to do, and I'm sorry, okay, Billy?"

"Okay, Harold," Billy said. "You want me to let you know when you're being stupid?"

"I don't think so."

During track practice with Billy on Monday afternoon, I thought about Billy's bicycle accident and the troubling events at Kate's house, and I became troubled and frightened all over again. I remembered little Mike Miller's bloody head slumped to one side in his tiny wheelchair and how Kate and his parents came to his rescue. I saw a vision of Billy underneath the wheel of a car, his crumpled bicycle locked in the automobile's grill. I closed my eyes to escape the vision.

"Are you sleepy?" Billy asked as he warmed up at the edge of the Lakeside track.

"No."

"Well, I'm ready to run my wind sprints, Harold."

"Okay, Billy. Be careful."

"Are you gonna shoot the gun or not, Harold?" Billy asked.

"Sorry. I forgot."

"That's okay, Harold. I forget stuff all the time."

"Runners, take your marks," I said. "Get set. Go!"

Billy's start was perfect. He came up low and fast, and every ounce of his energies seemed to flow through his legs. But his stride was terrible because of his right leg. He pulled it higher than he pulled his left leg, and he swung it out to his side. He swerved out of lane one, into lane two, farther out into lane three, and back across the cinders into lane one. Thirty yards down the track, he stumbled and fell to the cinders, picked himself up, and swerved the remaining twenty yards.

"You need to slow down when you're running track, Billy!" I yelled, running to see how he was.

"What?" Billy asked when we met.

"You need to slow down when you're running track."

"That sounds dumb, Harold."

"What sounds so dumb about it?" I asked, a little perturbed.

"I don't know. It just sounds real dumb, that's all."

"That's just great," I said. "I'm trying to teach you to take care of yourself, and you think it's dumb."

"I'm sorry, Harold," Billy said. "I thought you were

teaching me how to run track. I didn't know you were teaching me how to take care of myself."

I turned on Billy with a vengeance. "I'm trying to save your butt, Billy!" I grabbed hold of Billy's shoulders. "Do you think I want you to get run over by a car? Do you think I want you to break your neck jumping off your front porch? Do you think I want you to fall on the track and bust your head open on the cement curb? Do you think I want you to get hurt and turn into another Mike Miller? Do you think that's what I want?"

"No, Harold."

"Well, you're right. It isn't what I want."

"I'm sorry. I didn't know that's what you didn't want."

"Well, I don't want any of those things to happen to you," I said, dropping my hands from Billy's shoulders.

"Okay, Harold," Billy said. "I'll sit down on my bicycle from now on. And I won't jump off my front porch ever again. And if you want me to, I won't even run on the track anymore. I'll just watch you run. Is that okay, Harold? Will you like me again now, Harold?"

Billy enjoyed his bicycle. He enjoyed riding down the sidewalk, paralleling his bicycle's twin on the street. He couldn't do wheelies, but he could stand on the pedals and pump hard and sail over the bump where the sidewalk had buckled. He enjoyed the flight no matter how many times he made it; he always threw his head back and laughed each time he landed safely on the other side of the concrete ramp.

He enjoyed jumping off his front porch even more

than sailing across the sidewalk on his bicycle. Placing his right foot against the front of the house, he would sway until he had accomplished the exact rhythm he desired; then he would push away from the house and run across the porch as fast as he could. Usually his last step would be shy of the edge of the porch, and Billy would fly through the air like a wounded bird, falling to the ground spread-eagled, slightly injured, and crying sometimes. But sometimes he would hit the edge of the porch perfectly. Pushing away from the mark, he would move his legs through the air like an Olympic broad jumper and land close to the base of the old oak tree, standing, laughing, clapping his hands.

Now it seemed that Billy enjoyed running track more than just about anything. He enjoyed it more than riding his bike, more than jumping off his front porch. He enjoyed it because I enjoyed it, and he was willing to give it up to make me happy. In an instant, my anger slipped to shame. "I'm sorry, Billy," I said.

"Why are you sorry, Harold?"

"Because I was wrong. I want you to ride your bike standing up. I want you to jump off your front porch. I want you to run track with me. You deserve the chance to fall."

"You mean it, Harold?" he asked.

"I mean it, Billy," I answered.

I sat on the grass at the edge of the track and changed from my jogging shoes to my track shoes. Billy, wearing his old high-top sneakers, knelt beside me. He cocked his head to one side, reached out, and touched one of the cleats on the bottom of my shoes. I noticed the expression on his face. It was the same expression he wore the Christmas I got my new red bicycle. Billy wanted track shoes exactly like mine.

"Since you like practice so much, I'll ask your mom if you can get a pair of jogging shoes," I said.

"Just like yours?" he asked, pointing to my track shoes.

"Not exactly like these," I answered. "The cleats on the bottoms could hurt you if you stumbled or fell. What you need is jogging shoes."

"Just like your jogging shoes, Harold?"

"Just like mine, Billy."

Billy was ecstatic about getting a pair of jogging shoes, and he jumped and jogged all the way home from practice, stopping only to pick the best rose off Mrs. Damico's rosebush as we passed her house.

Both of us picked up our pace when Mrs. Damico stormed outside, yelling something in Italian that sounded something like the English Dad had used the day he banged his thumb with a hammer. Billy wanted to return the rose to Mrs. Damico's rosebush, but I convinced him that the rose was going to die anyway; and if we went back to Mrs. Damico's house, we might die as well.

Billy presented the rose to his mom as we entered his house. "This is a beautiful rose," she said. "You asked permission before you picked it, didn't you?"

Billy answered by not answering. He looked at me, giving me the responsibility of answering for him. It was one of his favorite defense mechanisms, so I was used to it. "Billy picked it on our way home from working out," I said. "It was just sitting there on the bush, waiting to be picked."

"I'm sure it was," Billy's mom said. "This rose looks a lot like the kind that Mrs. Damico grows."

"It looks a lot like her rose 'cause it is her rose, Mommy," Billy said. "You know what else? She hollered something funny at Harold and me."

"Why would that nice lady holler at you?" she asked.

"'Cause she's mean, that's why," Billy answered.

"Why do you think Mrs. Damico is mean, Billy?" she asked.

"'Cause Harold told me she was mean, that's why." This was one time I wished that Billy would have used his favorite defense mechanism instead of answering for himself.

"Harold didn't really tell you that, did he?"

"You bet he did, Mommy," Billy said, patting me on the back the way I patted him whenever he did something exceptional. "Harold says she's a mean old crap head."

"Is that what Harold says?" Billy's mom asked, looking at me. I decided it was time to use one of my favorite defense mechanisms, so I bowed my head and studied my zipper. "I think Harold is wrong this time. Don't you think you're wrong this time, Harold?"

"Yes, I'm wrong," I told my zipper. "Mrs. Damico is probably a very nice lady."

"Is she really, Harold?" Billy asked.

"In her own peculiar way," I said, still talking to my zipper.

Billy's mom let it go at that. It was one of the things I liked most about her. Unlike my mom, Billy's mom knew when to let it go at that. "Now that we've solved the mystery of the rose, what do you two have on your minds?" she asked.

"Racetrack shoes," Billy said. "I want some racetrack shoes."

"Racetrack shoes?"

"Jogging shoes," I said.

"I'll run better if I get a pair," Billy said.

"Real jogging shoes, Billy?" his mom asked.

"Racetrack shoes, Mommy. Red ones, just like Harold's."

"I had a feeling they had to be just like Harold's," she said.

"Please, Mommy, please. I want some this much." He spread his arms, stretched his hands for all they were worth. "Even more than this much."

"Well, I guess I'd better get you some jogging shoes before you stretch your arms out of shape," Billy's mom said, smiling at him. "We'll go shopping Saturday."

Saturday was slow in coming for Billy. Every day he asked me if it was Saturday yet, and every day I had to explain how many days were left. His high-top sneakers weren't good enough to train in anymore, and every afternoon he complained that his "dumb old shoes" slowed him down and made him fall. I was as happy as Billy when Saturday finally came.

Billy and his mom left for the store shortly after Billy and I returned from Saturday morning's training session. I took advantage of the rare solitude by practicing new ways to comb my hair so I could impress Kate Miller with my stylishness. I had never fretted over my appearance before. Prior to Kate there had been no one to encourage my primping. For the most part, there was nobody around to impress except Billy, and Billy, caring for me, cared little if I was impressive or not. Just as I was brushing the final stroke, Billy came bouncing into my room, grabbed my arm, and messed up that messed-up look I had painfully achieved.

"Look at all this stuff I got, Harold," he said, and he dumped a shopping bag full of loot onto my bed.

Billy's mom had outfitted him like an Olympic medalist. With the exception of cleats, there was everything a runner could possibly need scattered across my bed. He had a new pair of red jogging shoes, white athletic socks with red bands at the top, red track shorts, a red track jersey with white stripes, an athletic supporter, a red sweatband, and a red-and-white jogging suit. Every item was exactly like mine, with one exception. Billy's new athletic supporter was larger than mine, and I envied him for the second time in my life.

"Is it about time to get dressed for practice, Harold?"

"It's still a little early."

"Please, Harold, let it be time to get dressed," Billy

pleaded. "My new stuff is just sitting there waiting for me to put it all on."

"Okay, it's about time."

Decked out in his new attire, Billy had a greater enthusiasm for running than he had that morning; but since he was dressed like a track star, he was no longer content with warm-up exercises and noncompetitive races. He wanted more.

"I don't know what else you could do," I said after he completed his last wind sprint that afternoon.

"I want to do what you do, Harold."

"You've already done everything I've done so far today."

"I want to do what you do more than what you already did today."

I paused a few seconds to decipher what Billy had said. "You want to run the 400-meter run with me?" I asked.

"You got it, Harold."

"But I run four of them."

"I want to run four of them with you."

"But they're long and hard, and you'll get tired."

"Do you get tired, Harold?"

"Yes," I answered, and Billy smiled. "But you might get hurt, Billy. You might stumble and fall and cut yourself up on the cinders."

"What's so new about that?"

"But you might fall and hurt yourself even more than usual."

"I don't care, Harold."

"I care. I don't want you to get hurt."

"Please, Harold. Okay, Harold? Please. Please. Please."

I was getting to be a sucker for Billy's pleases. I looked at him in his new warm-up suit and realized that our fall from the tire could have been worse. He could have ended up in a wheelchair without the ability to speak or think or feed himself. He could have been like Mike Miller. What the heck, I thought. If Billy could do more, I'd let him, as long as he didn't interfere with my training. "You can't run a 400-meter race in your warm-ups," I said. "You'd better take them off."

"Hooray for our team," Billy sang as he shed his warm-ups. "Hooray for our team. Someone in the crowd is yelling hooray for our team."

"Listen, Billy," I said, grasping his shoulders so he couldn't turn his attention in another direction. "You're going to be in lane two, thirty yards ahead of me. I'll be in lane one, thirty yards behind you. I want you to try your very best not to come over into lane one; but to make sure neither of us gets hurt, I'm going to tell you to move over a little when I get close to you. When I tell you to move over a little, I want you to move a little to your right. Right is over there. It's that direction. You see, Billy, if you come into my lane when I'm close to you, one or both of us could get hurt. If we get hurt, we might not get to run for a long time. Understand?"

"I understand."

"Okay, it's test time."

"But I don't like tests, Harold."

"What lane are you in?" I asked.

"This lane."

"Not right now, Billy. What lane are you going to be in when you run?"

"Two, Harold."

"Good boy. Now, more than anything else, what are you not to do?"

"Pee in my new red track shorts," Billy said.

"Let's try that again," I said. "More than anything except peeing in your new red track shorts, what are you not to do?"

"I don't know, Harold."

"You're not to come into lane one. Got it?"

"Got it."

"Where is lane one, Billy?"

"Right there."

"Where is lane two?"

"Right there."

"Where are you to go when I tell you to move over a little?"

"Right over there."

"Very good, Billy," I said, patting him on his back. "Are you ready to run?"

"Is this still a test, Harold?"

"No, the test is over," I said. "Are you ready to run?"

"I'm ready to run, Harold."

"Get your rear in the air when I tell you to get set, and don't forget to come out low when I tell you to go." I was getting excited about Billy's first race.

"I won't forget, Harold."

"Do you have any butterflies in your stomach?"

"I don't think so," said Billy, lifting his track jersey and looking at his stomach.

"Are you nervous, Billy?"

"No, I'm not nervous."

"You aren't?"

"No, but I'll get nervous if you want me to."

"That's okay. Just run as fast as you can, and don't look back at me. Remember, it's okay to stop running after I pass you. I don't want you to get too tired your first race."

"What if you don't pass me?"

"What?"

"Nothing, Harold."

"Runners, take your marks," I said. I stretched my legs, backed into the starting blocks, and glanced thirty yards up the track at my competition, who was waiting for the next command from the starter. My butterflies had returned.

"Get set." Billy and I raised our rears in the air, and I focused on an old gum wrapper a few yards down the track. I didn't hear the shouts from the spectators in the empty stands. I didn't feel the wind that suddenly blew the gum wrapper into Billy's lane. I heard only my quiet breathing, and I felt only my dancing butterflies. Indeed, this had all the ingredients of a real race.

"Go!" I yelled, and both of us came up low and fast, cinders flying from under our feet.

It took ten yards farther than I had expected to catch Billy. He was doing exactly what I wanted him to do. He was pushing me. He stumbled once but continued to run faster than he had ever run. When I caught him, he moved a little to the right, straddling the faded white line that separated lanes two and three, and I passed him without incident or injury.

"Go, Harold, go!" Billy yelled as I moved ahead of him.

I never looked back after passing Billy, so I didn't know until I finished the race that Billy never quit running. I crossed the finish line, jogged to a stop, and kneeled on the cinders, breathing deeply. Several seconds later, I looked up to check on Billy, but I didn't see him on the first half of the track.

"Move over, Harold, 'cause I'm coming up fast," a voice behind me yelled, and I looked back just in time to brace myself as Billy stumbled across the finish line and fell over me.

"Are you okay?" I asked, picking cinders out of my skin.

"I'm okay. Are you okay?"

"I'm okay." It seemed that Billy and I were always asking each other if we were okay.

"Did I do good, Harold?" He searched my face for approval. "I only fell three times."

"You ran a good race, Billy."

"Thanks. My racetrack shoes helped a lot." Billy reached

down and dusted his new shoes. "When are we going to run again?"

"One race is probably enough for you today," I said. "Maybe you can run two races Monday, and then we'll increase the number each day. Don't you think that's a good idea?"

"Do you think it's a good idea, Harold?"

"I think it's a good idea."

"Then I think it's a good idea, too."

Every afternoon for the rest of the month, Billy and I ran at the Lakeside track. I could tell that I had improved, and I knew I had a shot at making the ninth-grade varsity. The realization of my dream was close, so close that I could almost hear the cheers from the stands.

Billy was getting better, too. He was faster than he was at the beginning of the month and had more stamina. He stumbled just as often as when he first began to run, but he didn't fall as much. By the end of the month, I was convinced that Billy could have been a contender had it not been for the funny way he stepped with his right leg, which caused him to stumble or trip every few strides. By the end of the month, Billy was a good runner, but he was a good runner with a bad leg.

Chapter 9

I awoke the Saturday morning before Monday's tryouts with sleep heavy on my eyes and a heavy decision spinning the inside of my head like an out-of-balance gyroscope. Should I run or should I rest? I wanted to run, and I wanted Billy to run with me, to push me. I wanted to get every last piece of practice I could get before the race against Jake Blake on Monday. But I also needed to rest, to relax and calm my nerves before the big event. I didn't want to chance a pulled muscle or a freak accident on the cinders this late in the game. I wanted to be fresh and injury free for Monday's practice. It was not necessary for me to run, because I was ready—I could feel it. But it was necessary for me to run because I wasn't sure if I could trust my feelings.

Tap, tap, tap. Tap, tap, tap. My neighbor was up to

his seven o'clock Saturday-morning tricks again. When I rubbed open my eyes and looked out the window, a cowboy was staring through the glass at me. I rubbed my eyes harder, and I looked out the window again.

The cowboy was still there, only it wasn't a cowboy at all. It was Billy wearing his ten-gallon cowboy hat, which stood a foot taller than his head and came down over his forehead to the tops of his eyebrows. He was still in his pajamas, but he was wearing cowboy boots, the toes of which were scuffed beyond the help of saddle soap. A holster and gun were strapped to his hips, and a real silver plastic sheriff's badge was pinned to his Mickey Mouse pajamas. All he needed was a horse.

"I left my horse tied up in your front yard, Harold," Billy said from somewhere beneath the brim of his hat.

"I hope he doesn't mess on the lawn."

"He won't mess on the grass, 'cause he don't eat nothing, not even hay," Billy replied. "Anyway, he ain't a real horse. He's really just my bicycle."

"Well, why don't you go put him back in the barn, Billy. He's probably sleepy from getting up so early on a Saturday morning."

"Silly Harold. Bicycles don't sleep."

"How do you know?"

"What?"

"How do you know bicycles don't sleep when no one is watching them?" I asked. "What else would bicycles do when no one is riding them?"

"Are you pulling my pecker, Harold?" Billy asked.

"Don't say that, Billy! Are you pulling my leg—that's what you're supposed to say."

"But you say it, Harold."

"I know I say it," I said. "But I'm not going to say it anymore because you might say it, and you might say it in front of my mom or your mom, or your Sunday school teacher, and then they'll ask who taught you to say such a thing, and you'll get a gigantic smile on your face and tell them that your friend Harold taught you to say it, and then they'll ask you if you're pulling their legs, and you'll say no, and then my dad will pull my legs off, and I'll be lucky if he stops with my legs. So, don't say it again, Billy, and I'm not pulling your leg."

"When are we gonna run track, Harold?" Billy asked, yawning.

"We aren't going to run today," I said, answering his yawn with one of my own.

"Why not?"

"Because I need to rest for Monday's practice."

"What are we going to play today?"

"Something relaxing," I said, "like Go Fish."

"Or maybe cowboys and robbers, huh, Harold?"

"We'll see, Billy," I said.

"What does that mean?"

"It means that we'll see if no one from my school is around before we play."

"Am I going to be the sheriff, Harold?" Billy asked.

"You're the sheriff," I answered.

Billy and I played cowboys, and every kid on the block between the ages of five and nine joined us. Fortunately, none of the guys from school pedaled through the neighborhood while we played that day. Had any of the guys from Lakeside Junior High seen me leading a band of ferocious five-year-old outlaws down my street in an attempt to escape a posse of second-graders led by a less-than-all-together sheriff, I would have been the joke of the school for weeks.

"Billy's team always wins," old lady Damico's grandson complained.

"That's because Billy has the loudest bang on the block," I said.

"And the most bangs, too," the kid said.

It was true. Billy could yell "bang" louder than anyone, and if he banged you once, he banged you a thousand times. Billy always made sure that the bad guys were stone dead. He didn't believe in wasting the taxpayers' money on trials.

"Well, I'm tired of being killed," old lady Damico's insolent little grandson said. "I want to be on Billy's team instead of yours. Billy's better at playing cowboys than you are, Smith."

"Don't call me Smith, kid," I said. "Go on over to Billy's side before I turn you over my knee and give you a good pop."

"You'd better not touch me, Smith," the kid said. "I'll tell my granny that you told me Santa Claus was dead."

"I never said anything like that, you little brat!"

"So what, Smith?" the kid replied, grinning. "My granny will believe me instead of you."

When old lady Damico's grandson left for Billy's side, I was an outlaw leader without any outlaws, and I didn't stand a chance. The good guys were too good for me. No matter where I ran to get away, at least one little kid would be waiting for me. They were not fast, but they could go anywhere. They could dart under parked cars, scoot through swing sets, drop out of oak trees. And they didn't care how dirty they got.

"I give up, Billy," I said, lying on the ground and breathing as if I had just run 400 meters full speed. I was surrounded by Billy's prepubescent posse, and they hovered over me like a flock of buzzards ready to tear the meat off my limbs. "I give up, Billy," I said again, surveying my predicament.

"I've had enough of his mouth," old lady Damico's grandson said. "Let's shoot the snot-faced, pig-nosed, sawed-off creep!"

"BANG, BANG, BANG, BANG, BANG, BANG, BANG, BANG, BANG, Harold!" Billy yelled, pointing his gun at my head.

"BANG, BANG, BANG, BANG, BANG, snot face!" Mrs. Damico's grandson yelled.

"BANG, BANG, BANG, BANG," another kid yelled, his gun halfway up my nose.

Billy and his posse had saved the taxpayers the cost of another trial.

"You're not supposed to shoot a guy when he gives

up, Billy," I said as the posse dispersed. "You're supposed to take him to jail so he can stand trial."

"What jail, Harold?"

"A pretend jail, Billy. It's just a game."

"That's why I shot you, Harold," Billy said. "I shot you because it's just a game, like running track. Right, Harold?"

Not right. Once upon a time track might have been a game to me, but it had evolved into something more. I had worked too hard for it to be a game. My legs had ached too often for it to be a game. My lungs had burned too hot too long for it to be a game. And most of all, my pride had suffered too much laughter for track to be a game. Track had become a proving ground for my ego, and no matter what it cost, my ego would be satisfied, like Billy's posse.

Monday finally arrived, and I wasn't sure if my nerves would last until practice in the afternoon. I flunked a pop test in algebra, stuttered my way through English, and daydreamed through Sherman's march to Atlanta. Had it not been for Kate, I think my insides would have shaken into a crumbled pile in my stomach and my skin would have collapsed from nonsupport.

"Try not to worry so much," Kate said as we ate lunch in the cafeteria. "You're going to run the best race you've ever run."

"Think so?"

"I know so," she said, taking my milk from my tray. "Milk might make you queasy," she explained.

"I'm already queasy."

"Milk might make you throw up."

"Take the milk," I said. "I feel like throwing up right now."

"Do you want me to watch?" Kate asked.

"What?"

"Do you want me to watch you run this afternoon?"

"Oh. No. No, thanks. I don't think so. But you can think about me if you don't mind. I'd like that."

"That'll be easy, Harold, because I think about you all the time," Kate said; and her smile calmed my insides, and the butterflies flew away.

Billy ran onto the track during my warm-up exercises that afternoon. He was decked out in his cowboy outfit, and the shadow cast by the brim of his hat dimmed everything but his smile.

"Who's your partner, Smith?" a grinning track-team member asked when Billy greeted me.

"You aren't supposed to be out here, Billy," I said, ignoring the question from my colleague.

"If you're looking for Indians to shoot, Billy, I saw a tribe riding off into the sunset." This second remark came from Danny Watkins, a kid who had played with Billy and me all our lives. He was our age, and he was a friend, except when he was trying to impress a group of ninth-graders. Strange how even the good guys in white hats can get caught up in the posse's fever.

"I don't shoot Indians, Danny," Billy said, hands on his six-guns and a frown on his face. "Me and Harold play cowboys and robbers, not cowboys and Indians. Ain't that right, Harold?"

Billy had the innate ability to shoot me down without drawing his guns. The knowledge that I played cowboys and robbers with the neighborhood urchins started a sweeping laughter that spread throughout the track team like a prairie fire, and I wanted to lie down on the track and be stampeded to death by a herd of track shoes.

"Why were all those boys laughing, Harold?" Billy asked after the crowd dispersed.

"Posses do that when they finally get their man," I said, and I quickly changed the subject before Billy took aim at me again with his six-guns holstered. "You know you aren't supposed to be on the track, Billy."

"Did you win the race yet?" Billy asked. He had a way of changing the subject, too.

"I haven't run."

"Good, 'cause I want to watch you win."

"Good, 'cause I want you to watch me win, too."

"That's two goods, Harold," Billy said. "Want to hear three?"

"I'm all ears, Billy."

"What?"

"I want to hear the third good, Billy," I said.

"I'm gonna run track at my special school."

"Your school is going to have a track team?"

"Yep, it sure is."

"Who told you that?"

"My coach told me."

"Your coach?" This was getting serious. All this time I had thought Billy just wanted to run so he could be like me. "But I thought *I* was your coach."

"Are you mad that I have another coach, Harold?"

"No, I'm not mad," I said, but I did feel a little jealousy creeping inside me.

"You know what else?"

"There's more?" I was still getting over what he had already said.

"A bunch more, Harold," Billy said excitedly. "I'm going to the Olympics."

"The Olympics!"

"The Special Olympics, Harold. I'm going to go to the Special Olympics. Ain't that a kick?"

"Wait a minute," I said. "You've got to qualify before you get to go to the Special Olympics. You'll need to place first or second in the state meet."

"Can I do that?"

"I don't know, Billy. It's going to be tough."

"But I'm tough, Harold. You said so yourself."

"Yeah, you are," I said. "I just don't want you to be too disappointed if you don't qualify to go to the Special Olympics. Okay?"

"Okay, Harold. I won't be too disappointed if I don't get to go to the Special Olympics, just like you won't be too disappointed if you don't win your race. Right, Harold?"

If any kid deserved to go to the Special Olympics, it was Billy. He had trained alongside me for weeks, and I had to admit he was good, despite his handicapped leg. But I also knew that there were hundreds of other kids with hearts as big as Billy's who wanted to be someone very special at a very special event. Maybe they'll give all the kids at school a ribbon for trying, I said to myself. Maybe Billy will get a ribbon, and maybe it will ease the pain of not being able to go to the Special Olympics. No matter what happens, Billy will get over it. He never stays down for very long.

Jake Blake tapped me on the shoulder. "Coach says it's time for us to run," he said. "You ready?"

"I'm ready, Jake."

"Good luck," Billy said.

"Thanks, Billy. Now, you'd better leave the track and sit in the stands."

"I'll cheer for you, Harold," Billy called over his shoulder.

The butterflies were back as Coach lined Jake and me on the track, but the butterflies picked me up, took my mind off the surroundings. I had drawn lane one. It was a good sign.

We backed into our starting blocks on the signal, lifted our rears in the air on the second command, and waited for the gun. Silence surrounded us as we held our positions. Even the wind, blowing up the legs of my shorts and into the folds of my athletic supporter, was quiet. My head was free of everything but running. I was ready.

"BAM!" The gun shattered the silence, and the race was on.

The weeks of training paid off. I knew it twenty-five yards into the race when I pulled ahead of Jake. There was no need to stride the backstretch to conserve energy for the final kick. I had the endurance to run with all my speed all the way around the oval track. My final kick was the fastest my legs had ever moved, and I crossed the finish line first. I was the fastest 400-meter runner at Lakeside Junior High, ninth-graders included. I felt great!

"Yea, Harold! Yea, Harold!" Billy yelled as he jumped over the fence that separated the track from the stands.

"You aren't supposed to be on the track," I yelled from the edge of the track, but he didn't hear me.

"You won, Harold!" Billy yelled. "You won the . . ." Suddenly, Billy's hat began to slide off his head. When he attempted to grab it, his right foot hit his left, and he stumbled. He was running too fast to right himself, and as he began to lose his balance, he reached out to me. It felt as if I had been hit by a bus as I broke Billy's fall.

Billy and I had fallen before. We had taken a hundred spills together after our tragic fall from the tire swing, and through all those spills we had picked ourselves up laughing. A hundred times the grass had cushioned the blows, rendering both of us injury free and happy.

This one hundred and first time was different. I fell

backward, and Billy fell on top of me. I cushioned his fall, but the concrete curb that bordered the inside of the track didn't cushion mine. I heard something snap when I fell to the curb, and I felt a sharp pain slice through the length of my body. The pain was followed by a numbing sensation, which was followed by nausea. It felt as though the butterflies had returned for the kill. Billy jumped to his feet, laughing. I wanted to tell him that it wasn't funny, but I vomited instead. "Why are you doing that, Harold?" Billy asked. "Why are you throwing up in my cowboy hat?"

Coach Barksley came to my assistance. "My arm hurts, Coach," I whined. "It hurts real bad."

"Everything will be fine," Coach said, "but I think I'd better get you to the hospital to have your arm checked."

"It's bad, isn't it, Coach?" I asked, and I looked at my arm for the first time since the fall.

It was bad. Coach Barksley knew it, and I knew it. My arm hung limp from the shoulder down. My hand was numb, and it was turning a deep shade of bruised blue—the same color that had spotted my neck the night Jennifer Jenkins and I had teamed up on the Sunday school hayride. My wrist was beginning to swell, and near my elbow, a huge lump had appeared beneath the skin.

"Try not to move your arm," Coach said.

Coach Barksley picked me up to carry me to his car, and my eyes met Billy's. "I'm sorry, Harold," Billy said.

Tears were streaming down his cheeks. "I'm sorry. Please
don't die, Harold."

"He isn't going to die," Coach said.

"You ain't gonna die, Harold?" Billy asked as Coach
Barksley carried me away. "You're going to be okay?" I
closed my eyes without answering and left Billy standing
alone at the edge of the track.

Chapter 10

Mom and Dad made it to the hospital just as the doctor had finished wrapping the cast that began above my elbow and ended at my fingers. "How are you feeling?" Mom asked.

"Track season is over for me," I said. I wanted to cry, but I didn't.

"Maybe you can run with a cast," she said.

"The doctor won't let me, Mom," I said. "And even if he would, the cast is too heavy. I couldn't compete."

"I'm sorry, son," Dad said as he rubbed my forehead. "I wish there was something I could do."

"It's over, Dad, that's all. All that work for nothing."

Billy was standing in the front yard when Dad steered our station wagon onto our driveway. Billy's hands were behind his back, and he was smiling. It really irked me that he could smile when my world had just crumbled.

It really irked me that he was so slow of mind that he didn't fully realize what he had done to me. All of those weeks of training for nothing. All of those dreams for naught. I wanted to jump out and break Billy's arm like he had broken mine; but I knew it would be a ridiculous thing to do. He would forgive me by nightfall, and by morning, he would have forgotten that it was I who had broken his arm. Man, how he irked me.

"Hi, Harold," Billy said as Dad opened the back door for me. "Guess what I got behind my back?"

"I don't care what you have behind your back," I said.

"It's a present for you, Harold," Billy said. "I made you a present because I almost killed you."

"You didn't almost kill me, Billy," I said impatiently, "but you did kill my dream."

"How did I kill your dream, Harold?"

"By doing this," I said, raising my cast into the air. "You broke my arm, you twerp."

"I made a drawing for you, Harold," Billy said, holding out his crude artwork. "It's a picture of your dog before he died. Remember old Spot? Remember when he used to chase our croquet balls? I put you in the picture petting Spot. See? I didn't think you'd want me in the picture, so I left me out."

"Good," I said as I pushed past Billy without taking his drawing.

"Please, Harold, I'm sorry."

"You go to hell!"

It was the first time in a long time that Dad let me

slide when I used bad language; but after he walked Billy home, he let me know that it would be a long time again before I could expect another free slide. I was sitting on my bed when Dad entered my room for our inevitable talk. I expected anger in his eyes, but there was only sorrow.

"Does it itch?" he asked. "Your arm, does it itch?"

"No."

"It will. It'll drive you crazy before too long," Dad said, sitting on my bed, changing his position before changing the subject. "Feeling better, son?"

"A little, I guess."

"It'll take time, but you'll get over it."

"I don't think I'll ever get over it," I said. "It isn't fair. It was Billy's stupid fault, not mine, and he isn't suffering at all."

"I think Billy is suffering, too."

"Well, I hope he suffers a lot."

"You want to know something, Harold?" Dad asked. "Most of the time you make me very happy; but some of the time you make me sad."

"Why, Dad?"

"You had a chance to do something much more important than making the varsity team, Harold, and you threw it away."

"Sir?"

"You were given the opportunity to forgive your neighbor. He broke your arm, but you broke his heart. You drove a stake through it. It's too bad you can't put a cast on a heart." Dad walked to my bedroom door and paused. "Sleep well, son," he said, and left.

I didn't sleep well. I tossed and turned all night. Every time I tossed, my cast would slide off my bed and hit the floor. Every time I turned, my cast would knock against the wall with a loud thud. If that wasn't enough, I dreamed weird dreams between tosses and turns. I dreamed I had fangs that dripped blood, and I was driving a croquet stake into my neighbor's heart while he tried to fend me off with a cross made of old wickets. If that wasn't weird enough, I also dreamed that Billy had me on the ground and was breaking my arm with a mallet while I attempted to drive him away with a wooden ball. Sometime in the early morning hours I finally forgot my dreams.

Billy didn't show up at the Lakeside track the day after my accident. In fact, he stopped coming to the track altogether, which pleased me. Every afternoon I would sit in the stands alone and watch my former teammates working out on the track below, and every afternoon I would become angry at Billy all over again. I no longer hated him for breaking my arm. I was just mad and didn't want to see him.

However, I would've liked to have seen Kate during my week of feeling sorry for myself. I wanted her to cheer me up and make me forget my troubles. She could do it simply by being close to me. But she hadn't been close all week. She hadn't even been in school. I called once, but her mother told me that she was with her brother and couldn't come to the phone. I didn't call again because I was getting kind of used to feeling sorry for myself, and it started to feel kind of good.

It was Friday, the week prior to the Lakeside Relays, and I was sitting alone in the stands watching Jake Blake run a 400-meter race against some ninth-grader who didn't stand a chance. I was feeling sorry for myself as usual, and I was hanging around the track to see if any of my old teammates would feel sorry for me as well. I was thinking about what I would say if Jake Blake asked how I was feeling. I was trying to come up with an answer that would make him feel real sorry for me. I couldn't think of anything, so I started reminiscing about the previous week, before my accident, when I was all excited about trying out for the varsity.

My thoughts were interrupted by the sound of a penny dancing at my feet against the metal stands. I hadn't noticed anyone enter the stands, but I had been so absorbed in my own little world that a navy battleship could have floated past me without my taking note of it. I looked up from the danced-out penny to see Kate Miller standing over me. "It's for you," she said.

"What?"

"The penny. It's for you."

"A penny for me?"

"A penny for your thoughts," Kate said, sitting next to me.

"I was thinking about last week," I said.

"You make it sound like it was a long time ago."

"It seems like it, but it also seems like it was a few minutes ago. It always happens when I think about the past. It doesn't make any sense, does it?"

"Sure," she said. "It seems like yesterday that we were all together—you, Mike, Billy, me—popping firecrackers in my backyard, and it also seems like it was a lifetime ago."

"You know something, Kate?" I asked. "When I'm sad, I sometimes start thinking about how close and far away something in my life is or was and shouldn't be or should. Does that make any sense?"

"It makes sense to me," Kate said as she picked up the copper coin and studied Lincoln's profile. "How's your arm?"

"Okay, I guess," I said.

"How's Billy?"

"Okay, I guess," I said. "How's Mike?"

"Mike ate a cricket one time," Kate said, ignoring my question. "I came upon him just as he had popped the poor creature into his mouth. The cricket's legs were sticking out of Mike's mouth, and when Mike wouldn't give up his prey, I tried to pull it out of his mouth. I ended up with the cricket's legs and nothing else. Mike had eaten the rest of it. My Mike. He did the strangest things sometimes."

"How is Mike?" I asked again, but I had a funny feeling I didn't want to know.

"I loved him more than I loved myself," Kate said. A tear fell from her face, flooding the Lincoln Memorial.

"How is Mike?" I whispered, feeling my stomach tighten.

"I loved him more than I loved my mom and dad," Kate said. "Is that a bad thing to say, Harold?"

"No," I said, and I knew the truth.

"Mike hurt himself," Kate said, holding my arm, tightening her grip as her eyes glistened in the sun. The penny slipped through her fingers and pinged quickly across the metal stands as though it were trying to flee the scene. "I wanted to talk to you because you'd understand," she continued. "He went away from me this morning, Harold. I was with him. I closed his eyes. He died this morning. My little Mike is dead."

I didn't say a word. I put my arm around Kate's waist and held her close. She allowed her head to fall lightly on my shoulder, and she held my free hand with both of hers. She never cried out loud. She just wiped her eyes every now and then and let her hands fall back into mine. I don't know how long we were there, but the track was clear of runners when Kate spoke.

"I'd better go home now," she said.

"Would you like me to walk with you?"

"Thanks, but I'd rather walk alone. I'll be okay." She smiled, hugged my neck, and whispered "thanks" in my ear.

As soon as Kate was out of sight, I ran as fast as I could from the Lakeside track to Billy's house. The cast on my arm slowed me down more than I thought it would, and twice I lost my balance and fell to the sidewalk. After each fall, I picked myself up and continued to run without worrying about my injuries. I had to get to Billy's house no matter how many falls it took. I had to get to Billy and fall before him on my knees.

For some strange reason, I thought about my dog, Spot, as I ran. Spot didn't have a spot on his coat, but Billy and I were only three when we named him. We were ten years old when Billy and I found him curled up lifeless on my back steps. I cradled Spot's head in my lap and cried like a three-year-old.

"Don't be dead, Spot," I said, tasting the salty tears at the corners of my mouth. "Please don't be dead."

"Poor Spot," Billy said as he knelt beside my dog and me. "Poor Spot and poor Harold." Billy reached down and pried Spot's dog tag from his collar, and the day of Spot's burial, Billy presented Spot's tag dangling from a chain to me. I wore that necklace for the next two years as a constant reminder of my love for Spot and, I realize now, of Billy's love for me. It had been my most prized possession at one time, and I wondered where it was now.

"Where is the picture you drew of Spot and me?" I asked Billy when he answered the door.

"It's in my room," Billy answered. "On my wall. Is that okay, Harold?"

"I want you to draw yourself in the picture, Billy," I said. "I want you to do it right now."

"Really?" asked Billy, smiling.

"The picture isn't complete without you, Billy. Spot,

you, and me. We went everywhere together. We were a team. Don't you remember?"

"I remember, Harold."

"After you draw yourself in the picture with Spot and me, I want it," I said. "Would you give it to me again? I want to hang it on my wall."

"It's always been yours, Harold," Billy said, "but there's just one thing."

"What's that?"

"I already drawed me in the picture, Harold."

If there is anything sadder than a child's funeral, I do not want to know what it is. Billy and I sat together at the church service for Mike, and we listened to the preacher as he tried to make some sense out of Mike's life and death. He did as well as anyone could do, I suppose. He chose his words carefully and looked directly at Kate and her parents so that it wouldn't appear that he was apologizing for little Mike's death. He spoke softly, but he spoke straight and threw no curves. I liked him, especially when he closed with words I had heard before:

" 'For now we see through a glass, darkly; but then face to face: now I know in part; but then shall I know even as also I am known.' "

Billy and I stood together at the graveside service facing Mike's coffin, which hovered over the opened grave on nylon bands. We stood behind Kate and her parents, who sat on little green folding chairs with the name of the funeral home stamped on the back of them. I wondered why the funeral home would deface chairs with bold white lettering as if they were army surplus equipment. Surely, no one would want to steal them. Who would want to sit in them?

"Mr. and Mrs. Miller, your son isn't in this coffin," the preacher said. "Kate, your brother is with God. Mike Miller is at peace and without pain."

"Mike ain't in that box, Harold?" Billy whispered.

"Mike isn't in that box," I said, not correcting Billy's grammar. "He's already in heaven."

Billy studied the sky as if measuring the distance between cloud layers. "Quick trip, huh, Harold," he said as he wiped his nose with the sleeve of his shirt.

Kate held her parents' hands as the pallbearers placed their boutonnieres on Mike's coffin. Billy stepped close to me, and I felt Spot's metal tag, which I had found again, brush against the skin beneath my shirt. The coffin was lowered into the ground, and little Mike Miller became a very fond memory.

Chapter 11

The Lakeside Relays were held the week following little Mike Miller's funeral, but I was not there to watch. I had something more important to do. Billy's track meet at his special school was scheduled the same afternoon. He was entered in the 400-meter run, and if he placed first or second in his event, he would qualify for the state meet. If he made it to the state meet and placed first or second, he would qualify for the International Summer Special Olympics Games. I had little hope that he would qualify for the Special Olympics, but I had a little hope that he might qualify for the state meet. It depended on how well he ran his first real race.

I surveyed the infield of the track as soon as I arrived at Billy's school. The 400-meter run was only minutes away, and I assumed that Billy would be warming up for his race. There were kids from several schools darting around the infield of the track like discharges of electrical energy: kids in green shirts, yellow shirts, blue shirts, pink shirts. Billy, however, was not among the energy and color of the track's interior. I could spot him in a crowd as easily as I could spot a rainbow after a storm.

I looked in the stands for my neighbor, but he wasn't there. I searched the perimeter of the track, and about halfway around the cinders, I spotted Billy sitting in the shade of an old tree. His head was so low that his hair brushed his knees.

"Don't you think you'd better warm up?" I asked, kneeling beside him. "The first call for the 400-meter run is only a couple of minutes away."

"I don't think I can run, Harold," Billy said. "I think I'm gonna throw up."

"It's the butterflies, Billy, that's all."

"Well, tell them to go away."

"Only running can make them go away."

"For sure?"

"Not for sure, Billy, but maybe."

"Just maybe?"

"It's a good maybe," I said. "Will you try to run?"

"I'll try, Harold," Billy said, slowly getting to his feet.

"There's something else I want you to try," I said as we walked onto the infield.

"Try what?"

"I've been trying all day to think of something that will help you stay on your feet so you won't fall during the race," I said. "Staying on your feet is the only chance you have."

"What can I do, Harold?"

"I have an idea, and if you listen carefully, maybe you'll get through this race without falling."

"Maybe I won't get sick. Maybe I won't fall. That's a lot of maybes for one race, Harold."

"All you can do is try. Now listen carefully. When you feel yourself losing your balance during the race, I want you to slow down and stop. As soon as you've stopped, I want you to get back in your starting position and start again. Come up low and fast like you always do because you'll have lost some time by stopping. Then, when you feel yourself losing your balance again, I want you to stop and start again. You'll have to be quick, and if you don't have to stop more than a couple of times, I think you'll have a chance to finish in the top three or four runners. What do you think?"

"I think I'm gonna be sick."

"There's the final call. No time to be sick. You'll have to run cold. Try not to pull a muscle. And listen to me, Billy. Remember to slow down when you feel yourself losing your balance. Remember to stop. Remember to . . ."

"I know, I know, I know, Harold." And Billy walked to the starting line.

"Get your rear higher, Billy," I yelled from outside the fence. The "runners, take your marks" and "get set" commands had been issued, and Billy, in lane eight, obeyed my order and lifted his rear a little higher into the air. "Remember what I've taught you, Billy. Winning is nice, but finishing is what really counts," I said, but I don't think he heard me.

"BAM!" The gun sounded, and the runners were off.

Billy jumped to an early lead because his start was tenfold better than the others'. His stride was good the first fifty yards out of the blocks as he pulled away from everyone.

A hundred yards out he began to lose his balance. He swayed to the right and his foot hit the cement curb on the outside of the track. He stumbled. A second more and he would have fallen.

"Slow down, Billy," I said to myself as I watched from the infield. "That's it. Slower. Now, stop! Get in your starting position. That's right. Now, go." He seemed to have heard my thoughts, and he followed my silent directions.

He came up low and fast just as the kid in lane three pulled even with him. A second later, the kid in lane three was falling back again. Billy's stride was fairly smooth and easy all the way into the backstretch, and then he began to lose his balance once again.

"Slow down, Billy," I yelled. "Stop. Billy. Get in your starting position. Great. Now, go, Billy, go!"

The kid in lane three was no longer a contender. Having figured out Billy's strategy, the boy had copied Billy's moves. Every fifty yards or so, the kid in lane three would stop, get in his starting position, and go again.

The kid in lane two gave Billy trouble all the way down the backstretch and into the curve. At the 300-meter mark, lanes two and eight were neck and neck. The kid in lane two pulled ahead in the homestretch. With fifty yards left in the race, lane two was a good two yards ahead of Billy, and it looked as though Billy would finish a strong second.

"Go, Billy, go!" I yelled.

Billy's final kick was as good as any I had seen at the Lakeside Junior High School track. It was a close finish, but Billy nipped the lane two runner out at the tape. My friend had started his first race three times, had finished it once, and had finished it first. He broke the tape, lost his balance, and fell to the cinders.

"Are you okay?" I asked, helping him to his feet.

"I'm okayer than I've ever been before in my whole life, Harold," Billy said. "Did you see me win that race?"

"I watched you every step of the way."

"You know what, Harold?"

"What?"

"Winning sure feels good," he said, brushing away the cinders that had stuck to his legs. "Even when it hurts a little, winning sure feels good."

Billy and I went home together after the track meet. I sat on my bicycle, pushing against the pavement with my feet while Billy skipped beside me, in back of me, backward in front of me, and a couple of times smashing smack into me.

I patted Billy on his back and told him what a great job he had done every time he asked how he had done; but in a way, I wished that he had placed second instead of first. The top two finishers in each event were invited to participate in the state meet, so a second place would have been as good as first except for the winning; and Billy would have known losing before he had known winning, which I have always thought was the best order to follow. I have met winners who can't stand to lose, but I've never met a loser who can't stand to win.

"Tell me again how I done, Harold," Billy said, narrowly missing a collision with my bike as he skipped from one side to the other in front of me.

"You were great, Billy," I said, feeding an ego already fat from my flattery. "You gave it everything you had. But there is just one thing you need to know."

"What one thing?"

"Your stride was uneven most of the way around the track, and your second start was a little sloppy."

"That's two things, Harold."

"I have one more."

"Another one!"

"I'm sorry, Billy, but you need to know this."

"Okay."

"Winning isn't everything," I said. "Finishing the race is more important than winning."

"I know," he said, "but is it as much fun?"

"Probably not," I replied, "but it's more important." Billy stopped skipping around my bicycle and paid attention to me for the first time since winning the 400-meter run. "I was very proud of you today, Billy."

" 'Cause I won the race, huh, Harold?"

"I was proud of you for finishing the race. I was happy that you won."

"I was happy for me when I won, too, Harold."

"That's fair, as long as you know that winning isn't everything."

"You already said that. Why do you keep saying that?"

"Because it's true. Because I want you to understand that finishing the race is more important than winning it. Because someday you're going to lose, and I want you to be prepared for it. Because the competition at the state meet is going to be tough, and there's no way you're going to win if you lose your balance even one time. Don't you see? Losing can be tough if all you care about is winning. I want you to know how to lose like a winner."

"But I already know how to lose, Harold," Billy said. "You don't got to worry about that."

"How do you know how to lose? You just won the 400-meter run at your first track meet."

"But I lost every bicycle race I ever was in," Billy said. "And I never won at marbles or hide-and-seek or climbing trees. The only time I won at chase was when you played like you fell down so I could catch you. I've always been a good loser, Harold. Don't you know that?"

I leaned over my handlebars and hugged his neck. Sometimes Billy was a real paradox. For someone so slow of mind, sometimes he was plenty smart.

Chapter 12

Saturday morning broke into my dream like an uninvited guest, crashing the party-for-two I was sharing with Kate Miller on a white, deserted beach on the sunny side of Narnia. It was a rude awakening: the sun in my face, my pajamas damp from the wet sand in my dream, and Billy sitting on my bed saying something about breakfast.

"Your mommy says that our breakfast is ready, Harold," Billy said, shaking me.

"What? Breakfast? Our breakfast?"

"Don't you remember, Harold? You told your mommy yesterday to fix breakfast for us today because yesterday you said that me and you were going to run at the track today. Don't you remember that, Harold?"

My mind was beginning to stretch and yawn. "What time is it, Billy?"

"The big hand is on the ten," Billy said, "and the little hand is on the . . . Tell me what comes after six again, Harold."

"It isn't even seven o'clock, Billy. It's Saturday morning, I'm awake, and it isn't even seven o'clock. Why is that, Billy?"

"Gee, Harold, I don't know," Billy said. "All I know is that the big hand is on the ten, and the little hand is on the, let's see, it's on the . . . the seven! Hey, Harold, it ain't even seven o'clock!"

"Way to go, Billy."

"Thanks," said Billy, and he knitted his brow. "Did you wet your pajamas last night, Harold?"

"No," I said, pulling the sheet to my chest. "Don't you think it's a little early for you to be here?"

"You said that you wanted to get an early start with my track practice."

"I didn't mean quite this early. The rooster hasn't even crowed."

"You always say that when I wake you up, Harold, and I've never ever even heard a rooster crow."

"It's just an old saying, Billy. You see, a rooster crows in the morning; and when you come over and wake me up and I say that the rooster hasn't even crowed, I really mean that it's too early to be awake. Do you understand?"

"Nope," Billy said. "How old?"

"What in the world are you talking about?"

"The old saying about the rooster. How old is it?"

"How do I know how old it is," I said. "It's an old saying, that's all."

"Is it as old as God, Harold?"

"Of course not. God is older than any old saying."

"How does God get that old and not die, Harold?" asked Billy.

"God doesn't look His age, and He never dies."

"How can He do that, Harold?"

"I don't know, Billy. I guess it's because He's outside the Earth's gravitational pull."

"Boy, Harold, you sure are smart."

"Well, maybe I'm a little smart," I said, smiling.

"And you know what else is old, Harold?"

"What?"

"Your breakfast."

Cornflakes don't get old, they get soggy. I think I would rather have cold eggs and warm milk than soggy cornflakes. No, maybe not. One thing for sure. You have to get to the table on time for breakfast, except for the orange juice, of course. Orange juice is good anytime. I can drink orange juice at room temperature without having to hold my breath or look the other way.

Billy ate the cornflakes that Mom had set at the table for him, and claiming that he liked soggy cereal better than he liked room temperature orange juice, he traded his warm juice for my soggy cornflakes. "Ummm, that was good," he said, licking away a limp flake that had stuck to his lower lip like soggy slime. "You ain't hungry, Harold?"

"No," I answered honestly. "My stomach's a little queasy."

"Probably because you wet your pajamas last night, Harold."

"What?" Mom asked as she picked up Billy's bowls.

"Nothing, Mom," I said. I felt my face grow warm. "Billy's just teasing, aren't you, Billy?"

"If you say so, Harold," Billy said. "Don't you think it's about time we got our butts in gear?"

"Where do you learn such words, Billy?" Mom asked.

"Well, Harold didn't teach me, that's for sure," Billy answered, and I breathed a sigh of relief. "Harold says that he don't teach me bad words. Harold says that when he says them, I just learn them all by myself." It was a short-lived relief.

"I guess it's about time for us to head for the track," I said quickly. "Let's go, Billy. See you around lunch-time, Mom." I felt her staring at me as I pushed away from the table.

"Harold?"

"Yes, Mom?"

"Did you put your pajamas in the dirty-clothes hamper?"

"Yes, Mom," I whispered, and I could feel the warmth growing on my face.

"Billy's waiting for you, so why don't you get your *rear* in gear," she said, and she kissed me on the cheek and whacked my rear at the same time.

When Billy and I reached the Lakeside track, I stepped on the cinders for the first time since my accident. It felt good to walk on them, and feel them crunch beneath my sneakers. I studied the oval track as though it were a favorite playground from my past, like the forest where Billy, Spot, and I used to romp when we were kids. I reached inside my shirt and stroked Spot's dog tag the way Billy and I used to stroke old Spot. It had been a long time since I'd thought about the good times the three of us used to have. I missed the good old days and, I realized now, I missed thinking about them.

"What are you looking at, Harold?" asked Billy.

"The past," I answered.

"Who's there, Harold?"

"We are, Billy, just like always."

"That's nice," Billy said, "but don't you want to coach me today?"

"Okay, I guess it's time to start," I said, saving the past for another day.

"What do I do first, Harold?"

"Stand in front of your starting blocks, Billy, as though you're getting ready for the race."

"Like this, Harold?" asked Billy, standing in front of the blocks.

"Almost," I replied. "Keep your arms limp and free

of tension. Shake your arms. That's right, but not so hard. Easy, Billy. Now, what are you thinking about?"

"I'm thinking about ice cream. Strawberry ice cream."

"You aren't supposed to be thinking about strawberry ice cream, Billy!"

"How about vanilla?"

"No, not vanilla or strawberry or chocolate!"

"I don't like chocolate, Harold. You know that."

"You're not supposed to be thinking about anything but the race," I said, taking a deep breath.

"But there ain't no race, Harold."

"Of course there is."

"There is?" asked Billy, and he looked at me as if I had gone mad.

"Every time you run, it's a race. In track, you run against the clock."

"I'm going to run against a clock?" Billy asked, convinced that I had lost my mind.

"Never mind. Just remember this: if you want to be extra good in track, you must make every practice a track meet and every run a race. Do you think you can use your imagination and make every run a race?"

"Sure I can," Billy said, smiling. "Pretending is easy. I always pretend that people want to play with me."

"Any questions, Billy?"

"Who's the boy in the blue shorts, Harold?" Billy whispered. "Do you know his name? I've seen him somewhere before."

"What are you talking about?" I asked. "There's no one on the track but us."

"Shhh, Harold, he'll hear you," Billy said. "In that lane over there, standing in front of his starting blocks and shaking the nerves out of his hands. What's his name?"

"Oh, that kid," I said, glancing at Billy's imaginary competitor in lane four. "I don't know his name, but I've seen him run."

"Is he fast?"

"Pretty fast."

"As fast as me?"

"It'll be a close race," I said, "but I'm afraid he has the edge on you right now."

"Why does he have the edge on me right now?"

"Because he's concentrating on the race instead of you," I said. "Runners, take your marks. That's it, Billy. Just relax. Get set! Get your rear a little higher. Remember to come out of the blocks low and fast. Ready? GO!"

Billy had a fantastic start, and his stride was smooth and fast the first fifty yards out of the blocks. Then it was the same old story, the same sad song. He began to sway as his right foot went higher into the air. He stumbled, righted himself, stumbled, righted himself, stumbled, and fell. He picked himself up from the cinders and began to run again.

His stride was good again. He fell again at 200 meters but got up quickly. At the 300-meter mark, he was running as fast a race as he had ever run. With 50 meters left to run, he stumbled and went down to the cinders a third time. A third time he picked himself up and ran toward the finish line.

Five yards shy of the finish, Billy's right foot came down hard on his left, and my neighbor came down hard on the track. He cried out, and tears washed the cinder dust from his eyes. I wanted to shout "Stop, Billy, stop!" but I said nothing as Billy pushed himself to his hands and knees and crawled toward the tape. He finished the race.

"Not too good, huh, Harold?" Billy said, thumping cinders off his bloody knees.

"You would have run a great race if you hadn't fallen."

"It wasn't my fault," Billy said, frowning. "The kid in the green shorts tripped me."

"The kid in the green shorts tripped you?"

"You saw it, too?"

"No, I didn't see him trip you. Besides, I thought the kid was wearing blue shorts."

"That was a different kid, Harold. Didn't you see me race against two kids?"

"Billy, let's stop pretending for a minute, okay? Sit down on the grass so I can talk to you seriously."

"Are you mad at me?"

"I'm not mad at you," I answered. "I'm just concerned about you running in the state meet."

"Why, Harold?"

"I don't think you're ready for it."

"Then get me ready for it. You're the coach, ain't you?"

"Aren't you, Billy," I said, correcting his grammar.

"Don't get weird, Harold," Billy said. "Just get me ready for the race. Tell me what to do, and I'll do it."

"Don't fall down when you run."

"What?"

"Don't fall down when you run," I said again. "The kids you'll be running against are good, and they don't fall down when they run. If they're as fast as you are and if they don't fall down when they run, they're going to . . ."

"They're going to beat the up-yours out of me," Billy said.

"Something like that."

"What are we going to do, Harold?" Billy asked. "My old foot just won't do what it's supposed to sometimes."

"I know you can't help it," I said, patting Billy on the back. "And it's okay if you fall and lose the race."

"It is?"

"I've told you that a hundred times."

"Then why are you worried?"

"I'm worried because you might not want to finish if you're losing really bad," I said. "If you're so far behind that people are laughing at you, you might want to stop. You can't do that, Billy. You've got to finish the race. If you give up during the race, you might give up after the race."

"I'll finish the race no matter what, Harold," Billy said. "I promise I will."

"You have to. If that foot quits this race, it might think

it can never run again. And that would be a tragedy. Win, lose, or draw, that foot must finish whatever it begins."

"You know what that foot wants more than anything, Harold?"

"What?"

"It wants your foot to be its friend," he said, smiling.

I picked my right foot up to my ear and listened to its soul. "What's that you say, foot? Tell Billy's foot what? Okay, foot, I'll be happy to."

"What did your foot say?" asked Billy.

"My foot said that it will lend your foot a jogging shoe anytime."

Billy threw his head back and laughed. I had always loved to hear him laugh. Grabbing his bad foot, he attempted to bring it to his ear; but he was unable to get it too close to his head. Making sure that the foot would hear, Billy shouted to it: "WHAT'S THAT YOU SAY, FOOT? TELL HAROLD WHAT? OKAY, I'LL TELL HIM FOR YOU!"

"What did your foot say, Billy?" I asked, smiling.

"It said to tell you that your jogging shoe ain't big enough to fit no more, but thanks anyway."

I threw my head back to laugh, but Billy let go of his foot at the same time, allowing it to free-fall into my lap. Immediately, my laughter turned into a cry of agonizing pain as I doubled over, knees against my chest, and rolled on the grass. "Hey, Harold," I heard Billy yell from the opposite end of a long barrel, "let go of my foot. Your knees have got my poor foot and you're shaking my leg every which way." A minute later I released Billy's foot from my intimate grasp, and I picked myself up to my hands and knees. "Hey, Harold," Billy said. "You look like a horse."

"A gelding," I said as my body finally escaped its pain.

"Is that a racehorse, Harold?" asked Billy, and I threw my head back and laughed the laugh I had been denied a few minutes earlier.

Billy and I went back to work as soon as our laughter died. He backed into the starting blocks for his second 400-meter run of the day, raised his rear in the air, and came out low and fast. He ran a good seventy-five yards before he fell the first time, but he fell four more times before the race was over. As he crossed the finish line, I shook my head from side to side and wondered what could be done to keep Billy on his feet for a mere 400 meters.

"Why don't you teach him to walk before you teach him to run?" someone shouted from the stands.

"Why don't you mind your own . . ." I stopped short when I saw who had spoken. Kate Miller looked down from the stands at me. Her head was tilted a little to one side, and she teased me with a smile.

"What were you saying, Harold Smith?" she asked.

"I was asking what you were doing here on a Saturday morning," I lied.

"I thought that's what you said," Kate replied. "I'm here to watch Billy practice."

"I can already walk," Billy suddenly yelled to Kate. "Tell her, Harold. Tell her that I can already walk. Who does she think she is?"

"Billy! You're being rude!"

"No, he isn't," Kate said.

"Yes, I am, 'cause Harold said so," Billy replied.

"You just don't understand what I mean, Billy," said Kate.

"I don't understand what you mean either, Kate," I said.

"Wait a minute, and I'll explain." And Kate made her way down the stands to the track. She was wearing white shorts, white sneakers, and a white sleeveless blouse that ended where her stomach began. Her stomach was smooth and soft and small: the stuff that dreams are made of. It was refreshing to note that our navels were alike. She had an inny, and I had an inny. Something to build on there, I thought.

"She sure is pretty, ain't she, Harold," Billy said.

"She's beautiful, Billy," I replied.

"Hello, guys," Kate said as she approached us. "Would you like for me to explain what I meant when I said that Billy needs to learn to walk before he learns to run?"

"No," Billy said.

"Yes," I said.

"Yes," Billy said.

"Two out of three isn't bad," Kate said, and she turned her attention to Billy. "Billy, I want to show Harold something that might help him coach you better. Would you please walk down the track a few steps and then walk back to us?"

"How many steps?" asked Billy.

"How about twenty," Kate said.

"I can't count to twenty."

"How high can you count?" she asked.

"I can count to ten real good."

"Great," Kate said. "Walk ten steps down the track and then walk ten more steps. That's twenty."

"Is it, Harold?" asked Billy.

"Ten steps and ten steps are twenty steps," I answered.

"That's neat," and Billy began to count his steps. "One, two, three, four, five, six, seven, eight, nine, ten. One, two, three, four, five, six, seven, eight, nine, twenty. I did it, Harold. I counted to twenty."

"Do you see what he's doing with his right foot?" Kate asked as Billy walked back toward us. "He's picking it up higher than his left foot for some reason."

"He's done that since he was four years old," I said. "It's a lot worse when he runs."

"Okay, let's watch him run," Kate said.

"Billy, I want you to run to that little tree down there," I said as he approached us. "Do you see the one I'm talking about?"

"I see the one you're talking about, but don't you want me to run to the big one over there instead?"

"Just run to the little tree and back."

"But I got to pee, Harold, and that little tree ain't big enough to hide behind."

"Can't you hold it for a minute, Billy?" asked Kate.

"Billy isn't a very good holder," I said.

"That's right," Billy said. "I might wet my pants like Harold wet his pajamas last night."

I looked on the ground for a gun with which to shoot myself. Seeing none, I looked up in the trees for a rope with which to hang myself. Where are guns and ropes when you need them?

"You wet your pajamas last night, Harold?" Kate asked with a wicked little smile.

"I didn't wet my pajamas," I said. "Billy ate breakfast with me this morning, and I spilled my orange juice on myself."

"He did not," Billy said.

"I did, too," I said.

"He did, too," Billy said.

"Two out of three isn't necessarily good, Harold," Kate said.

"Run, Billy!" I said, and Billy headed for the old, familiar oak tree at the 300-meter mark.

Kate and I didn't say anything as we watched Billy run toward the tree. As always, Billy lifted his right foot higher into the air than he lifted his left foot. As always, he fell to the cinders before reaching his destination.

Billy made it to the tree shortly after his second fall. He brushed the cinders from his knees and elbows and eased around to the back side of the oak. "Can she see me peeing, Harold?" Billy asked, peeking around the tree.

"I can't see you, Billy," Kate said.

"I asked Harold."

"She can't see you, Billy."

"Are you the only one in the world Billy trusts?" asked Kate.

"When it comes to urinating behind trees, I'm the only one he trusts."

"I guess that's fair," she said.

Billy jogged back to where Kate and I were standing. "You've seen him run, Kate," I said. "Now, how do we solve his problem?"

"Weight," Kate said.

"Wait for what?" I asked.

"Not wait," Kate said. "Weight."

"Wait a minute," Billy said. "I'm getting all mixed up."

"Stand in line," I said. "I've been mixed up since I met her."

"W-e-i-g-h-t," Kate said.

"Oh," I said. "Weight, as in pounds, Billy, not wait as in stand still."

"What line do you want me to stand in?" Billy asked. "I'm still all mixed up."

"Well, hold me a place in line, Billy," I said. "I still don't know what a weight has to do with this."

"If Billy is lifting his right foot higher than he lifts his left foot," Kate said, "it makes sense that if we place just the right amount of weight on his right foot, he'll begin to lift it evenly with his left foot. Understand?"

"I understand," I said, "but there's one major draw-back."

"What's that?"

"The extra weight," I answered.

"Wait a minute," Kate said. "Maybe I'd better stand in line with Billy because now I don't understand what you're talking about."

"The extra weight that Billy would be carrying would slow him down," I said.

"But it probably wouldn't be more than four or five pounds," Kate said. "How much could that slow him down?"

"At least a half second," I said, "and maybe even a whole second. A second added to Billy's time would put him completely out of the running in the state meet, which would knock him out of the Special Olympics."

"How much time does Billy lose each time he falls?" asked Kate.

"At least a second, probably more."

"And how many times does Billy fall in one race?" asked Kate.

"Three to five times."

"That's three to five seconds. As Billy's coach, I guess you have a decision to make, Harold. Which costs Billy more time: falling down while he's running a race or carrying some extra weight on his right leg?"

"I guess it's worth a try," I said.

"Is that okay with you, Billy?" Kate asked.

"Whatever Harold says is okay with me," Billy replied. "How are we going to make my foot wait?"

"Billy asked a good question," Kate said. "What are we going to use for a weight?"

"My ankle weights," I answered. "They weigh two and a half pounds each, and one of them should be perfect to start with."

"Ankle weights?" Kate asked. "Are they those funny-looking gadgets you wore around your ankles at school every day?"

"Funny-looking? I didn't think they were funny-looking."

"That's because you never saw yourself from the back while you were wearing them."

"Who cares?" I asked. "How many girls go around studying a boy's backside?"

"You'd be surprised."

"Well, I don't care if I look funny from the rear."

"You're right," Kate said. "It really isn't very important."

"Besides, people talk to you from the front, not from the rear," I said, and I caught myself pulling my pants up in the back.

"You're right, Harold," Kate said. "Don't worry about it."

"I'm not worrying about it," I said, and I turned and walked in Billy's direction. Before I had taken the second step, I had the uncomfortable feeling that Kate was staring at my backside. I turned to her once again. "Do you really think my rear is funny-looking?"

"I never said that your rear is funny-looking," Kate said. "I said that those gadgets you wore to school made your feet look funny from the back. Your rear looks just fine."

Strange how we notice people going as well as coming. From that day forward, I began to spend almost as much time not facing my mirror as I spent facing it.

Kate volunteered to wait with Billy at the track while I went home to get an ankle weight, and when I returned, I found Kate and Billy lying on their backs, their hands folded behind their heads. They were searching the sky for animal clouds—pointing out zebras and kangaroos before the wind blew their shapes away.

"A unicorn, Billy," Kate said.

"Where, where?"

"Over there. Look over there. See?"

"I see, Kate. I see." And they smiled as the unicorn danced and somersaulted in front of the wind. It was good seeing Kate smile. Even when the wind finally caught the cloud, she smiled at the unicorn's memory.

"Did you see that unicorn cloud, Harold?"

"I saw, Billy."

"Great, huh, Harold?"

"Great," I replied as I looked at Kate.

"Now that you're back, I guess I'll let you and Billy

get back to practice," Kate said as she stood and brushed the seat of her shorts. "I've kept you from practice long enough."

"You can't go, Kate," I said. "Billy and I need you."

"Why do you need me, Harold?"

"Why do we need her, Harold?"

"We need Kate because we can always use another coach, Billy," I said. "We need you, Kate, because we can always use another friend. What do you say? Will you help?"

Kate grinned. She looked at me and then at Billy. She cocked her head a little to one side, and her lips parted into a smile. "What's the pay?" she asked.

"Five percent of Billy's winnings."

"Make it ten and you've got a deal," she said.

"Agreed," I said. "Kate is the newest member of Billy's coaching staff. Now, let's get this weight strapped to your right ankle, Billy, and get back to practice."

"Thanks," Kate said as we strapped the weight to Billy's ankle.

"For what?"

"For helping me see animal clouds again."

There was a morning session and an afternoon session that day. During the morning session, Billy ran only fifty-yard sprints so the weight on his ankle could be adjusted after each run. He started with the full two and a half pounds of lead shot in the canvas ankle weight, and after each sprint, a small amount of lead was added or taken out of the ankle weight. After eleven sprints that morning and a two-hour lunch break, we, as Billy's coaches, felt that he was ready for the afternoon session.

The afternoon session was the real test: a full 400 meters, and Billy would be carrying the extra weight all the way around the track. As Billy backed into the blocks, I felt the butterflies pumping their wings in my stomach. "Last chance," I said.

"What, Harold?" Billy asked.

"This is your big chance," I said. "Are you ready?"

"I'm ready, Harold."

"Runners, take your marks. Get set. Go!"

Billy had a poor start, but it was the start of the best race he had ever run. His stride was smooth, and he kept his balance all the way around the track. Not once did he fall. Not once did he stumble.

The ankle weight checked his speed a little, but Billy was much stronger than I had imagined. He ran the track like a champion, and crossed the finish line five full seconds ahead of his best time.

"It works, Kate!" I shouted as we watched Billy jog back toward the finish line. "The ankle weight works. You're a genius."

"Thank you, Coach Smith," Kate said, smiling.

"Of course, Billy isn't strong enough to win," I said. "Not yet, anyway. He needs to build the strength in his right leg. His overall stamina needs work, and his start is still too sloppy."

"At least I didn't fall down, Harold," Billy said. "That's good news, ain't it?"

"That's the best news of all," I said. "Now we can concentrate on training and stop worrying about you falling down and cutting yourself to pieces. We know you can finish. Now, let's give you a shot at winning."

"Hooray, Harold!" exclaimed Billy. "I'm gonna win!"

"Do you know what it means if Billy places first or second at the state meet?" I asked, as if I had just realized that the impossible was possible.

"What?" Kate asked.

"My friend will go to the International Summer Special Olympics Games," I answered. "Billy will be an Olympian."

Chapter 13

The ankle weight improved Billy's performance in the 400-meter run, but there was still a lot left to work on when we ran out of time. The day Billy had to leave for the state track meet arrived. He was to travel by bus to the host city that afternoon, spend the night, and run his event at two o'clock Saturday afternoon. There was nothing more his coaches could do. Billy would have to win with what he already had..

Our station wagon was waiting in the Lakeside parking lot when Kate and I got out of school that Friday afternoon. Mom was taking Billy and his parents to meet the bus so they wouldn't have to leave their car in the lot overnight. Mom and Billy's parents were sitting in the front seat. Part of Billy was in the backseat and part of Billy was hanging out of the window, and he waved to us as we approached. "Hi, Harold. Hi, Kate."

"Hi, Billy," said Kate.

"Hi, Billy," I said. "Get back in the car so Kate and I can get in, okay?"

"Okay, Harold," he said, backing into the backseat.

"Kate and I will be thinking about you when you run tomorrow," I said as Mom drove toward Billy's special school.

"We'll be cheering you on to victory. What do you think about that?"

"I think I want you to go with me, Harold," Billy said.

"I wish I could go with you, too, but I can't. Only the athletes and their parents can ride the bus, and I don't have a way to get there."

"But you're my coach, Harold."

"I'm just your coach during practice, Billy. The coach from your school is your coach during track meets. I explained that already. Don't you remember?"

"I remember," Billy said, and he slumped down in the seat. "That don't mean I like it very much."

"Are you getting the butterflies about the track meet already?" I asked.

"No."

"Are you getting the butterflies about riding the bus and spending the night without Harold?" asked Kate.

"Yep."

"You're afraid to ride the bus and spend the night without me?" I asked.

"I ain't afraid, Harold!" Billy snapped. "I just got the butterflies about it, that's all. That's right, huh, Kate?"

"That's exactly right," she said, and Billy scooted a little closer toward Kate. "They'll probably go away soon after you get on the bus."

"They will?" asked Billy.

"Sure, they will, Billy," I answered.

"I was asking Kate," Billy said.

"I think so, Billy," Kate said. "You'll probably forget all about the butterflies by the time you get a couple of miles outside of town."

"I'm going out of town?" Billy asked.

"He'll never make it," I whispered to Kate.

"He has to make it," she whispered back.

"Couldn't you ride your bike to my race, Harold?" Billy asked, leaning toward me once again.

"It's too far, Billy."

"Couldn't you take a taxi?"

"Still too far."

"But what if I need to talk to you and you're not there, Harold?"

"You can phone me, Billy," I answered. "I'll give you the exact numbers to dial. Is that okay?"

"If you say so, Harold. You'll talk to me on the telephone like you do when I'm at my house?"

"Just like you're next door," I said. "Anyone have a pen and a piece of paper?"

"I do," Kate said, and she pulled them from her purse.

"Okay, Kate, my phone number is . . ."

"I know your phone number, Harold," she said and began to write.

"You know my phone number? How do you know my phone number?"

"I just know it, that's all."

"If you know my phone number, why haven't you called me?" I whispered.

"Because girls aren't supposed to call boys, that's why," Kate whispered back.

"Says who?"

"Says my mom."

"Oh."

"Here's your note with Harold's phone number, Billy," Kate said. "Now, put it where you won't lose it."

"I ain't going to lose it," Billy said. "I'm going to put it right here, where nobody will take it."

"Not in there, Billy!" I said, as Billy stuffed the note in his underwear. "Put it in your sock."

"But nobody will take it out of here, Harold."

"I'm sure they won't, but nobody's going to take it out of your sock, either."

"If you say so," Billy said, stuffing my phone number inside one of his socks.

"I wrote my number on the note, too, Billy," Kate said, "just in case you want to talk to a girl for a change."

"Thanks, Kate," Billy said, and he hugged her neck.

The trip home from Billy's school was long and quiet— long because it was quiet, I guess. Even with Kate sitting beside me, I felt a little empty and a lot lonely.

Billy called collect that night—five times. By the end of the first telephone conversation, I was sure that Billy was going to finish the race the next day; but by the end of the fifth conversation, I was just as sure that he would not. I would have had a restless night had it not been for Kate's telephone call shortly after Billy's fifth one. Billy had called her, too, and Kate assured me that my friend would finish his race.

I slept soundly Friday night and on into the daylight hours of Saturday morning. There were no fingers pecking on my window, arousing me from sleep. There was no familiar, muffled voice calling through the glass of my window, asking if I was still asleep, asking if I was dead, asking if I was going to wake up. A second of panic knotted my stomach when I awoke at ten o'clock to silence and an empty window. "Where's Billy?" I asked the morning sun.

"What did you say?" Mom asked from the hallway.

"Nothing, Mom," I answered, realizing the day, the time, the whereabouts of my neighbor.

"You'd better hurry and get dressed," Mom said. "Kate called a few minutes ago, and she's on her way over. I was just about to awaken you."

"What? She's coming over here?"

"She's on her way," answered Mom. "What would you like for breakfast, or brunch?"

"Forget it, Mom. There's no time to eat," I said, jumping out of bed and looking into my mirror.

"You should eat something, Harold."

"Toast. I'll have a piece of toast and a glass of milk. Is it okay if I eat in my room while I'm getting dressed?"

"That's not a healthy way to eat," Mom said. "If you'd like, I could feed you, like I did when you were a baby."

"Come on, Mom. Don't start with the baby stuff. It's too early in the day for that, and I'm too old."

"You'll always be my baby, Munchkins," Mom said.

"Please, Mom, I thought we were over the Munchkins talk," I said, throwing my pajamas under the bed. "Will you entertain Kate if she gets here before I'm dressed?"

"Consider her entertained. Your father and I will sing her our old favorite. Remember 'Shoo Fly, Don't Bother Me'?"

"Oh, great. Then she'll think you're as weird as I am."

"Who thinks you're weird?" Mom asked.

"Practically the entire world," I said, and Mom didn't reply. I guess she agreed with them a little.

"I'll bring your toast and milk to you as soon as it's ready," Dad called from the kitchen.

"Thanks, Dad," I said, and I began to mumble to myself as I looked into the mirror and dressed. "Look at that hair! I could fry an egg in that grease. No time to wash it. I'll wear my baseball cap. Look at that baseball cap! I could grow a lawn on it. A clean shirt. Great. Now for the jeans. Jeans? Where are my stupid jeans? Here they are, stupid. Stupid cast. I can smell it from here. Where did I hide Dad's cologne? Cologne? Come here, cologne. Got ya! Take that, cast. And that. You, too, armpits. Take that. And that and that and that. Darn, I think I overdid it. I look okay from the front, now what about the back? Look at that butt! I think the dumb thing sticks out too much, and these jeans don't help. Maybe if I smooth them out a little. . . ." I looked over my shoulder into the mirror and began to press my blue jeans against my rear, rubbing harder and harder, faster and faster. Just as I thought I was making a little headway, I saw my father staring at me from my bedroom doorway.

"What are you doing?" he asked, toast and milk in hand.

"Dad! Dad? What? What, Dad? What do you mean?" I always asked for an explanation when I didn't have one of my own.

"Why are you rubbing your rear?" He never let me down. He could always explain exactly what he meant.

"The seat of my pants is wrinkled."

"The seat of your pants is wrinkled?"

"And they're sticking out a little."

"And they're sticking out a little?"

"Yes, sir."

"Who cares?" Dad asked.

"I care."

"Who goes around looking at the seat of your pants, Harold?"

"I do, Dad," I said, taking the blame for Kate Miller. "Sometimes. When there's a mirror handy."

"Here's your toast and milk," Dad said, setting my breakfast down on my bedside table and keeping a safe distance from me.

"Is Harold dressed?" I heard Mom ask from down the hall.

"Almost," Dad answered, smiling.

The doorbell rang as I gulped down my last swig of milk. I heard the sound of Kate's voice traveling down the hall from the living room as my father greeted her at the front door. I pressed at my jeans once again and joined the other half of Billy's coaching staff in the living room.

It was almost a three-hour wait before Billy's scheduled run at two o'clock that afternoon, but his coaching staff managed to pass the time constructively. We played dominoes, which was Dad's idea. We played Go Fish, which was Mom's idea. Kate signed my cast, which was my idea. After signing her name, Kate drew a heart around her signature, which was her idea. When my parents went outside to grill hamburgers, Kate and I were left alone in my house, which was no one's idea, and the best idea of all. We sat so close on the sofa that our bodies touched whenever we inhaled at the same time, and I tried to time my breathing to coincide with hers.

"Do you really think he has a chance to win?" Kate asked just as I had worked up the nerve to put my arm around her waist.

"Who? Oh, Billy. I just want him to finish the race. That's enough."

"What do you think he's doing?"

"Right now?"

"This very minute."

"He'd better be warming up. It's almost time for his race."

"Do you know what I think he's doing right now?" Kate asked. "I think he's thinking about us. Isn't that kind of neat? We're thinking about Billy and Billy's thinking about us."

"He probably was, but he isn't anymore," I said, glancing at Mom's clock. "At least, he isn't if we're the coaches we think we are."

"What do you mean?" Kate asked.

"It's less than a minute before the gun sounds," I said. "Billy should be at the starting blocks, and he should be thinking of nothing but the race."

"Runners, take your marks," Kate whispered.

"Get set," I added.

Mom's clock chimed twice, and Billy was off and running.

At two o'clock that afternoon, my neighbor ran three simultaneous 400-meter runs: the race he ran in Kate's head, the race he ran in mine, and the race he ran on the track.

"Well, it's history now," Kate said, breaking the silence. "Are we ready to declare?"

We had made a pact. We had agreed that when the imaginary race had been run in our minds, we would let each other know the outcome at the same time. On the count of three, we would declare how Billy had fared in his race. One finger meant that he had won, and two fingers meant that he had not.

"One, two, three," Kate said, and one of Kate's fingers fell across one of mine. Out of the three races Billy ran that day, we knew he had won two of them.

Billy's bus was due to arrive back at his special school around eight o'clock that Saturday night. When Kate left to go home, I went to my room and propped myself against the headboard of my bed. I read, played solitaire, put together puzzles; but mostly I stared at the drawing of Billy, Spot, and me that was tacked on my bedroom wall.

"Billy's back," Dad said suddenly from the doorway. "Your mother and I are going to pick them up. Are you coming, Harold?"

"Would it be okay if I waited on his front porch swing, Dad? I'd like to talk to him when he gets home."

"Sure," Dad said. "We'll be back in a few minutes."

It was such a calm night outside that the only breeze I felt was the one I created by setting Billy's front porch swing in motion. It was quiet, too, except for the squeaking of the swing's chain against its hooks. Floating with the motion of the swing, I tried not to think about Billy's race; but it was too quiet and too calm. I watched Billy run the race again in my mind. It was a different race than the one I had watched him run that afternoon with Kate. Sitting in the swing, I watched him stumble and fall three times, and the third time he didn't bounce back. Instead, he pulled his scraped and bleeding body from the cinders and crawled off the track. He didn't finish the race.

I welcomed the itch inside my cast as it made its way from my fingers, up my forearm, and just out of reach of my fingertips. I allowed the itch to creep up my arm unhampered by my fingernails. My concern for Billy's not finishing the race shrank with the swelling of the itch inside my cast.

I rested my cast across my legs, and its weight reminded me of Mom's blue photo album lying open upon my lap. I looked at Billy's name printed in large block letters across my cast, and I thought about a picture of us when we were three. We were climbing a ladder to a backyard slide. Me first, and Billy two steps below, holding a hand under my rear in case I were to slip.

Billy had come a long way since the first day he ran track with me, and I was glad that I had coached him. But I wondered how far he would have come had we still had the backyard slide when we were four, instead of a tire hanging from a tree. I would probably be running on the 1600-meter relay with him, and we'd be competing with each other for Kate Miller's affections.

My cast slid across my lap when I swung backward. I caught my broken arm before it knocked against the seat of the swing, and I placed the cast in my lap again, holding it with my good arm. Having a cast on my arm was an aggravation sometimes, but my uninjured arm was getting stronger because of it.

Our station wagon's headlights swept Billy's front porch, and I reached into the shadows of the yard and broke a thin but sturdy switch from Billy's oak tree. In the time it took for Billy to walk from my driveway to his front porch, I had attacked and destroyed the itch inside my cast, and I was prepared to hear what had happened at the state track meet.

"Hello, Harold," Billy said, and I could tell by the way he spoke that all had not gone according to plan.

"Hi, Billy," I said, motioning for him to join me on the swing. "You look a little sad."

"That's because I am a little sad, Harold."

"Do you want to tell me what happened?" I asked, feeling sure that I already knew.

"I didn't win my race, Harold."

"That's okay, Billy," I said, and I asked the question I dreaded asking. "Did you finish it?"

"Of course I finished the race," Billy said indignantly. "Don't you know that you're supposed to finish no matter what?"

"You finished the race?" I asked again.

"I finished the race," Billy answered again, "but I didn't win."

"You finished the race!" I said, giving Billy a big hug. "You finished the race!"

"You ain't hearing what I'm saying, Harold."

"You aren't hearing what I'm saying, Billy."

"Yes, I am, too!" said Billy. "But you ain't hearing what I'm saying. I didn't win the race, Harold."

"That's okay," I said, releasing my bear hug hold on him. "You tried your best, and you finished the race. That's what really counts. It isn't the end of the world because you aren't going to run in the Special Olympics."

"But I *am* going to the Special Olympics, Harold," Billy said.

"What did you say?"

"I said that I'm going to the Special Olympics."

"You didn't win the race, did you, Billy?"

"I already told you that."

"How far away from winning were you?"

"About this far," Billy said, indicating a three-inch space between his thumb and index finger.

"You were three inches from winning?"

"Yep, but I didn't win."

"You came in second place, didn't you?"

"Yep, but I didn't win."

"You came in second place, Billy!" I said, giving him another bear hug. "Don't you know what that means?"

"Yep, it means I didn't win."

"It also means you won, Billy," I said, getting up from the swing and dancing around the front porch. "First and second place in each event at the state meet go to the International Summer Special Olympics Games. You're a winner, my boy. You're an Olympian!"

Chapter 14

The practices following the Special Olympics state meet were hard on Billy and his coaches, especially Billy. He pushed himself to the limit every day, and every day he improved. My friend the Special Olympian was ready to meet the competition on any given day on any given track. He was in top condition. His stride was smooth and even, and his final kick was fast and strong. He came out of the blocks as well as he had before the addition of the ankle weight, and most important, his ankle weight seemed a part of him, as if he had worn it all his life. During the final two weeks before the International Summer Special Olympics Games, I had made an important change in Billy's track uniform. I had replaced his jogging shoes with a pair of track cleats, to which he had adjusted in one practice outing. With the addition of the ankle weight, Billy had acquired a balance he had never known.

With the addition of the track shoes, he had gained some valuable speed. Billy, the Olympian, was ready.

"How do you feel?" I asked as we walked home from our last practice before the Special Olympics.

"I feel fine," Billy said. "How do you feel?"

"I feel fine, too," I said. "You leave tomorrow for the Special Olympics, you know."

"I wish you was going to be there, too, Harold," Billy said, and I saw that he was getting a little sad at the prospect of going to another track meet away from home without me.

"But I'll be with you in spirit," I said. "I'll be thinking about you the entire time. Even when you're on the bus on the way there, I'll be thinking about you."

"That ain't as good as being there, Harold," Billy said. "It ain't that good, is it?"

"No, it isn't that good, Billy," I answered as we walked up Billy's sidewalk toward his front porch, where our moms were swinging in the swing, "but it's a lot better than not being there at all."

"Would it make you happy if Harold went to the Special Olympics and watched you run, Billy?" his mom asked suddenly. It surprised me that she would ask such a question when she already knew that I couldn't go. The Special Olympics were three states away and were going to last four days. It cost too much to go. It was as simple as that.

"It would make me real happy, Mommy," Billy answered. "Could you go with Harold, too?"

"Would you like that, Billy?" she asked.

"Sure, Mommy."

"Would you really like to go to the Special Olympics, Harold?" Mom asked.

"I'd love to go, you know that, Mom," I said. I was getting cautiously excited.

"Do you want to go to the Special Olympics badly enough to keep the station wagon another year or so, Harold?" she asked.

"What are you talking about, Mom?"

"You've always wanted your dad to buy a regular car instead of a station wagon, haven't you?"

"Sure, but what has that got to do with me wanting to go to Billy's Special Olympics?"

"A couple of weeks ago your dad decided that it was time to trade in the station wagon," Mom said, "and he decided that it might be a good idea to buy a regular car this time, since you've always wanted one."

"You're kidding," I said. "He's really going to buy a regular car instead of another station wagon? What kind of a car? What color? Not green. Don't let him buy a green one."

"A red one," Billy said.

"No, blue," I said. "Let's get a blue one."

"Yeah, let's get a blue one," Billy said, "with a red top."

"How badly do you want to go to Billy's Special Olympics?" Mom asked.

"I already told you, Mom. I want to go more than anything."

"More than getting a new blue car with a red top?" she asked.

"I don't understand what you're talking about, Mom."

"Okay, enough of the mystery," she said, smiling. "Your father suggested that we do one of two things. We can either trade the station wagon in on a new car now, or we can keep the station wagon until next year and all take a trip to Billy's Special Olympics. We decided that it should be your decision."

"That's no decision," I said. "We can keep the station wagon for ten years!"

"Are you going, too, Mommy?" Billy asked. "And Daddy?"

"We'll be there, too, Billy," she answered.

"There's something I failed to mention," Mom said.

"What's that?"

"Your father called the Millers," she said. "Kate is going, too."

"You're kidding."

"We thought both of Billy's coaches should be there with him," Billy's mom said.

"You're kidding?"

"She's not kidding, Harold," Billy said. "Everybody's going to watch me run."

Billy didn't mind boarding the chartered bus that would take him to the International Summer Special Olympics Games because he knew that our parents, Kate, and I would be two days behind him in the station wagon, and all of us would get to see him run. He smacked everybody smack on the mouth before he entered the bus. Just before the bus pulled away from the curb, Billy stuck his head out of the window. "Hey, Harold, is it okay if I call you collect if I get the butterflies before you get there?" he asked.

"Sure it is, Billy," I said, and for the next two nights I waited close to the telephone for Billy's calls, but none came.

Everyone was at my house early the morning we were to leave for the International Summer Special Olympics. I don't remember our station wagon ever being as crowded as it was that morning, not even when Billy and his parents vacationed with us. However, going to the Special Olympics was different. Four adults, two kids, and luggage enough for everyone taxed even the capacity of our large, three-seater station wagon. Making certain that every available bit of space was used effectively, Dad had taken an hour and a half to pack the vehicle; and when all of us had squeezed inside, we were jammed shoulder to shoulder.

I, for one, didn't mind the cramped conditions at all. As a matter of fact, I decided that a station wagon was the only way to travel. Mom and Dad were in the front seat; Billy's parents were in the middle seat; and Kate and I, dressed in shorts, T-shirts, and tennis shoes, were pressed side by side in the far backseat amid boxes, paper sacks, and luggage. For the first hour of our twelve-hour drive, Kate tried to keep her leg from resting against mine, but she silently gave up the struggle sixty miles out of town and let her leg rest gently against mine.

"Wake me when it's time for lunch," Kate said. "I didn't sleep well last night. Excited, I guess." She laid her head on my shoulder, yawned quietly, and entwined her arms around my left arm. She nuzzled her face against my sleeve and went to sleep.

The white of the highway's broken center line flashed by our station wagon in an unsuccessful attempt to keep time with my heartbeat, which was pounding so hard and so loud that I was sure Kate could feel its rhythm against her face and Mom could hear its thumping all the way in the front seat. I glanced down at Kate, but her head was not bouncing from my arm with every beat of my heart; and Mom hadn't turned around in the front seat to check on the strange, thumping noise coming from the rear of the wagon.

Trying not to wake her, I gently pulled one of Kate's hands from my arm and held it in mine. I laid my head against the back of the seat again, closed my eyes, and relaxed. Normally, I would have slipped slowly into one of my secret dreams; but my present situation was better than a dream, and I decided to stay awake as long as possible to soak up the warm rays of reality.

I don't remember falling asleep, but I remember waking to the smell of bologna. Not my most pleasant awakening. I opened my eyes to the awful sight of something that resembled mayonnaise dripping down the front of my shorts. "What are you doing?" I asked before my eyes had focused.

"I'm giving you a sandwich," Kate said. "It's lunchtime. It's bologna or nothing."

"I'll take it," I said. Dreaming about deserted beaches and starry nights always made me hungry, even for bologna.

After lunch, Kate and I played cards. We played Go Fish for at least two hours, and then we switched to a game called Hearts. It was a lot more fun than Go Fish, especially since I had never played before and had an excuse for losing every hand. By the end of the fourth game I was tired of losing and Kate was tired of winning. We settled back in our seats and talked and napped for the rest of the afternoon.

Twelve hours and forty-seven minutes after backing out of our driveway, our station wagon of weary travelers ascended the tall bridge that carried us across the Mississippi River and into Baton Rouge, Louisiana, the home of Louisiana State University, host of the International Summer Special Olympics Games. It was the time of day when it was not really light outside and not really dark: light enough to see from Billy's house to old lady Damico's house once your eyes were adjusted, but too dark to get permission to ride a bicycle down the street.

I surveyed the stunted scenery far below us as our station wagon reached the summit of the bridge. Buildings skyrocketed without reflection along the murky shore, and ships began to melt into the water. Behind the buildings and to the right was the Louisiana State University campus.

I could see the outline of the entire athletic complex with all its buildings and athletic fields huddled together in one vast corner of L.S.U.'s extensive grounds. Tiger Stadium, the bowl-shaped football stadium, dominated the complex, and it was there that the Special Olympics' opening ceremonies were to be held that very night. Flanking Tiger Stadium were the baseball stadium, the basketball stadium, the indoor swimming complex, the field house, and the track stadium where Billy would compete as an Olympian in the 400-meter run. I felt the butterflies beginning to spread their wings. On that college campus, Olympic history would soon be in the making, and my friend Billy would be a part of it.

"Are we going to make the opening ceremonies, Dad?" I asked as we pulled into the parking lot of our motel.

"We'll make it. According to the city map, Tiger Stadium is about five miles from our motel, and we have an hour before the ceremonies begin."

"Don't worry," Kate said to me when Dad went inside the motel's office to register. "An hour will give us plenty of time."

Wrong. An hour did not give us plenty of time. Cars were everywhere, and every one of them was headed for Tiger Stadium and the opening ceremonies. Depression swept over me like a humid mist, dampening my spirits and clouding my mood. Since the minute I had learned I was going to the Special Olympics, I had looked forward to the night of the opening ceremonies. In my dreams I had watched my neighbor and friend march around Tiger Stadium's infield to the cheers of thousands of spectators. In those dreams he had picked me out of the multitude, and I had heard my name over the roar of the crowd. "Hello, Harold," Billy called. "Do you see me down here?"

"I see you, Billy," I said aloud in the station wagon.

"What?" Kate asked.

"Nothing."

"We'll make it," she said and squeezed my hand.

We turned on a tree-lined boulevard at the third traffic light and continued at our same old pace. I was convinced we wouldn't make it in time to see the final leg of the torch bearer's relay and the lighting of the Flame of Hope at the top of the stadium. I became more agitated, more nervous. My legs moved back and forth, and my knees knocked against each other with each inward movement—the way they did whenever I desperately needed to go to the rest room, and the way they did whenever the preacher was ten minutes into the second overtime period during the Sunday-morning sermon.

"How far are we from the stadium?" I asked, breaking the silence.

"I don't know," Dad said, "but we can't be too far away."

"He's right," Kate said. Her face was pressed against her window, and her breath had created a ghostly outline of her features on the glass. "I can see the stadium lights from here, and they look like they're fairly close."

"Where?" I asked, leaning over her.

"Over there," Kate said, moving from the window and pointing past the nose print she had left behind on the glass. "Look between the space in those two trees."

I wiped Kate's nose print from the glass, searched the space between the trees, and saw a piece of the night glowing in the distance. Kate was right. Tiger Stadium was not far away.

We were getting close. Following the right turns of the cars in front of us, we pulled onto the parking lot of Tiger Stadium, a stretch of concrete so vast that the shopping center that had usurped the entire forest where Billy, Spot, and I used to romp would have fit in one corner. There were cars everywhere, stretched out in long, neat rows.

When we finally parked, I had to restrain myself from running ahead of the others. We entered the stadium and climbed five inclining ramps beneath the stands before reaching the level on which our seats were located. When we walked into the open air of the bowl-shaped athletic arena, I had to stop and catch my breath. I wasn't winded from the climb—I was awed by the spectacle that greeted all of us under the lights. My eyes scanned the entire bowl. Tiger Stadium had a seventy-five thousand seating capacity, and there was standing room only.

"Can you believe this?" I asked. "There's not a seat left in the house. What a turnout!"

"They've come to see Billy," Kate said, and as she spoke, the stadium lights began to dim. "Hey, why are the lights going out?"

"The torch bearer must be coming into the stadium," I said.

We located our seats as the stadium grew darker. Soon there was just enough light to see the steps at the edge of the aisle and the outline of the stadium across the football field. Seventy-five thousand people grew silent in anticipation of the Special Olympian who would carry the torch to ignite the Flame of Hope at the top of the stadium, behind us. When the darkness at the west end of the stadium was suddenly broken by the light of the torch bearer, the silence in the stadium was broken by an outburst of cheers from thousands of fans. It was spontaneous. It was exhilarating. It was emotional.

The girl who carried the torch ran once around the stadium's infield before making her way into the stands; and when she entered the stands, she ran up the aisle adjacent to our row of seats, taking two steps with each step she took. She held the torch high above her head, and the light from its flame danced across her smiling face to the rhythm of the silent breeze that swept down into the gigantic bowl. Her leg brushed Kate's shoulder as she passed our row of seats, and she paused long enough to say, "I'm sorry, miss."

"That's okay," Kate said, but her reply was two steps too late.

Seconds later, the torch bearer dipped the torch, letting its flame touch the enormous bowl at the top of Tiger Stadium. Instantly, fire shot into the night like fireworks on the Fourth of July. The crowd roared and kids squealed with delight. Little Mike would have liked this night, I thought to myself.

"It's great, isn't it?" Kate said, shouting into my ear. I looked at her and smiled, but I didn't reply. She put her arm around my shoulder and squeezed me, like pals do when they think the same thought.

The overhead lights flooded the stadium seconds after the Flame of Hope was lighted. The band that shared the stage with the dignitaries at one end of the field began to play, and the march of the Special Olympians was under way.

What can I say? Fantastic! Beyond fantastic. It was spectacle and ceremony and inspiration all rolled into one. What a high I felt watching six thousand special athletes from around the world march with their respective delegations around Tiger Stadium's infield. Each delegation stood straight and tall on the football field as it ended its part in the parade; the colors of the uniforms rippled down the yard markers from delegation to delegation.

Our state's delegation entered the stadium close to the end of the march. They were dressed in white jogging shoes, red warm-up pants with white stripes down the outside of the pants legs, white warm-up shirts with red stripes down the outside of the sleeves, and solid red caps. Each one of them carried a miniature American flag in his hand and waved it with elated enthusiasm upon entering the arena. I scanned the 150 flags as they passed in front of our viewing area.

"There he is," I heard Billy's mom say.

"I see him," Dad said.

"I see him," I said, and I waved to my friend, who looked up into the stands and waved to me and seventy-five thousand other people who loved him, too.

It was a magnificent sight when every member of every delegation from around the world was assembled on the football field. Special Olympians covered every square inch of the field. The band suddenly stopped playing, and one of the dignitaries from the platform stage walked to the microphone. She stood silent for a moment, contemplating the majesty of the moment, I am sure. Then she began her speech.

"Is she a movie star, Dad?" I asked.

"Not exactly," he answered. "That's Eunice Kennedy Shriver."

"Who's she?"

"She's a very nice lady, son," Dad said, adding, "even if she is a Democrat."

I didn't know much about politics, but I knew enough to know that if my dad thought a Democrat was nice, that person must really be special. "Why is she going to speak?" I asked.

"She founded the International Summer Special Olympics Games," Mom answered.

Mrs. Shriver paused after closing her speech in order

for the applause to lessen. Just prior to the silence that followed the applause, she stepped up to the microphone again. She thanked the crowd for its enthusiasm and thanked the athletes for the honor of allowing her to honor them. "A class act," Kate said, and I agreed.

Mrs. Shriver began to give a long list of introductions as she called the names of the dignitaries seated on the platform stage; several musical numbers from a popular band followed. By the beginning of the third musical number, every athlete on the field had started dancing, gyrating to the fast rhythm of the song. It was a wild and exhilarating and fun night, and I hated to see it come to a close.

"When will I get to talk to Billy?" I asked as we flowed with the crowd down the ramps on our way out of Tiger Stadium.

"Tomorrow," Dad answered.

"But I wanted to talk to him tonight. He needs to know we're here, don't you think?"

"Billy is probably very tired," Dad said.

"But he's probably depressed because he hasn't heard from me."

"It's almost ten o'clock, and Billy needs his rest," Dad said. "You may phone him in the morning. That's all, Harold."

There is something strange about fathers. One always knows when they've said all they're going to say on a given subject. "Yes, sir," I said, and I flowed with the crowd toward the exit in silence.

"When does Billy run?" Kate asked as we drove toward the motel.

"The last day of the track events," I answered.

"That's a long time to anticipate a race," she said.

"That's true," I said, "but we'll get to spend some time with him tomorrow. That should help him some. I can already hear his excitement when he answers the phone in the morning."

Chapter 15

I was up at six o'clock, but it didn't do any good because Dad wouldn't let me phone Billy until after breakfast, which was around eight. It would've been an unbearable wait had it not been for Kate. She, too, was up by six and phoned the room where Dad and I were staying to see if I wanted to take a walk while everyone else got dressed.

Louisiana was beautiful in the morning hours in summer. Of course, the Memphis city dump would have been lovely if Kate Miller was walking beside me through the trash and holding my hand. We walked around the motel's pool twice without saying a word, and then Kate led me out to the end of the diving board. "We're not going in with our clothes on, are we?" I asked.

"I thought you liked to be different," Kate said.

"I don't necessarily like it. I just am, that's all."

"That's one of the reasons I like you," she said.

"You like me because I'm weird?" I asked.

"I like you because you're different," she answered. "Billy isn't even your brother, and you love him as much as I loved Mike. That's different, and I like you for it."

"So you think you've got me all figured out?"

"I don't think I'll ever have you all figured out, Harold Smith," she said, smiling. "You're kind of weird sometimes, you know."

"So I've been told."

"There is one other reason why I like you so much," Kate said. "I like you so much because you like me so much." She stepped close to me, pressed her body to mine, wrapped her arms around my neck, and kissed me right on the mouth.

I felt the earth move beneath us, or maybe it was the diving board. I felt my face flush. I felt my toes flush. I felt my loins flush. My blood was pumping faster than my thoughts, but my thoughts were gaining fast.

Flabbergasted! That's the word Mom always used when she was shocked speechless by something. Not being one who was shocked speechless by anything, I was never quite sure what flabbergasted meant; that is, not until Kate flabbergasted me on the diving board. Five minutes later, she flabbergasted me again when she kissed me on the way to breakfast.

Kate and I joined the others for breakfast a little after 8:00, and I was ready to phone Billy by 8:25. Mom admonished me for sucking down two over easy eggs in two not so overly easy bites and told me that I could not be excused from the table until I had finished my milk and had wiped the yolk from my chin. I gulped down my milk, wiped my chin, and headed for the pay phone in the lobby.

"He's coming to the phone," I told Kate, holding my hand over the telephone receiver. "The phone must be in the hall. Anyway, the house parent is going to Billy's room to bring him back to the phone. Wait. What? Billy? It's Harold, Billy. This is Harold."

"Hello, Harold. This is Billy."

"Great! Great! How've you been?"

"I've been fine. How've you been?"

"Great! Great! Kate is here with me. We saw you last night at the opening ceremonies."

"I didn't see you."

"I was there, Billy. We were there," I said, trying to dispel his loneliness.

"I was there, too, Harold."

"I know. I know. We saw you. You looked great in your red-and-white warm-up uniform."

"Thanks."

"Have you missed me, Billy?" I asked, knowing his answer.

"Harold, I got to go now."

"What?"

"I'm living in this great big house and some boys who

live here with me want me to teach them how to play Let's Go Fishing in the Clear Blue Lake, Harold. Bye, Harold." Click. The phone went dead.

"What? Wait, Billy. Wait a minute."

"What happened?" Kate asked.

"He hung up."

"He hung up?"

"He hung up."

"He was probably so excited that he didn't know what he was doing," Kate said.

"No," I replied. "He said he had to go visit some kids down the hall."

"It's okay," Kate said. "We're going to take him to lunch, and you can talk to him then. He'll probably start jumping up and down when he sees you coming." She sensed my sudden depression. Never in our lives had Billy not wanted to talk to me.

Between breakfast and lunch all of us toured the university's campus. Although it didn't cheer me up, the tour did take my mind off my thoughts of Billy's finding another best friend and Billy's not needing me anymore. The campus was huge and interesting, and there were students all over the place. At least half of the students were girls and at least half of the girls were beautiful. There is nothing like God's scenery to lift a boy's spirits. It was a good tour, and I wouldn't have minded extending it had the clock on L.S.U.'s tower not struck twelve and reminded us that it was time to meet Billy at his dormitory.

Billy's dormitory was a tall, modern structure that faced a parking lot of bicycles and little cars with canvas tops, and it backed against a small, shaded lake with peopled blankets strewn on its banks. The foyer opened into a huge room, complete with several groups of seating areas and an enormous fireplace at the far end. It was one of the most beautiful rooms I had ever seen. It was as beautiful as the funeral home where Mike Miller's services were held, only the dormitory's room was more beautiful because it was alive with kids who were very much alive.

We searched the large room for Billy, but he wasn't there. I walked away from the group and looked out a window onto the lake. It was after twelve o'clock, and Billy wasn't waiting for me in his dorm. I felt as though I had lost my best friend because I had the feeling that I had.

"What's the matter with you?" asked Kate.

"Billy wanted to talk to his new friends instead of to me when I phoned this morning," I confessed. "And he never phoned me collect while he was here and I was still at home."

"So?"

"So, he isn't here. He must want to be with his new friends instead."

"So?"

"What do you mean, 'so'? Billy is my friend."

"You've told me several times that you want Billy to have other friends," Kate said.

"Sure, I want him to have other friends," I said. "But . . ."

"But what?"

"Billy can have other friends, but he belongs to me!" The second I said it, I wished I hadn't said it. The second after the second I said it, I realized how really dumb it sounded. "That isn't what I mean," I said. "I just don't know how to say what I'm talking about. I guess it's because Billy has never been away from me before."

"But you've been away from Billy," said Kate.

"That's different," I said. "No, really, it's different because Billy's different. When I'm away from Billy for a few days, I know I'll feel the same about him when I return. But I'm not so sure about Billy. He doesn't remember like we do."

"You're afraid he'll forget you, aren't you?"

"I need him, Kate," I said, admitting it out loud for the first time. "He makes me strong."

"He'll never forget you," Kate said, "but you've got to give him some room."

"What do you mean?"

"Mike could never grow, Harold, but Billy can," Kate said. "You've got to let him grow."

"Hi, Mommy!" I heard Billy's voice from the doorway. I turned around and watched as he ran to his mom and hugged her neck. "Where has everybody been this morning? I've been waiting outside. Where's Harold? Why didn't Harold come, too? Where's Harold, Mommy? Why didn't he? . . ." And he spotted me.

When Billy had rubbed away the last ray of the morning sun from his eyes, his familiar smile broadened. It was the very same smile that had left me on its way to the Special Olympics. "Harold!" he screamed, and Billy ran straight for me with outstretched arms. "It's me, Harold. It's Billy."

I braced myself for the impact, but I didn't brace myself for Billy's embrace. He was two full strides from contact when his feet left the carpet. He continued to run, his feet pumping air like a broad jumper heading for the pit. The force of Billy's airborne body ramming my stationary self scared the breath out of me. The impact lifted my feet off the floor of the foyer and slammed me down onto the carpet. "Thump!" Even the carpet cried out as the weight of our two bodies crashed down upon it.

"Are you hurt, Harold?" Billy asked, sitting on my stomach and checking my cast for cracks. "Do you feel okay, Harold?"

"I'm not hurt," I answered, gasping for breath, "and I feel better than I have all day."

"Me, too, Harold," Billy said, and he kissed me full on the mouth.

"How are you, Billy?" I asked.

"I'm hungry," Billy answered. "How are you?"

"I'm hungry, too," I said.

"Come on, everybody," Billy called. "Let's go eat."

We took a detour on the way back to the dormitory from lunch because Billy wanted us to see something "fantastic, unbelievable, greater than great." I didn't know what it was, but truthfully, I wasn't impressed at Billy's hyperbole. Over the years I had learned not to be easily impressed by Billy's impressions because Billy was so easily impressed: with things, with people, with life in general. Certainly I was excited that he was excited, but I was certain that I wouldn't be impressed.

I was impressed. It was fantastic. It was unbelievable. It was greater than great. Olympic Town was every superlative Billy had given it. It was a little town, a village where the special athletes came between events to relax and have fun. A sidewalk meandered through the community of brightly colored tents: big tents: not as big as circus tents, but a lot bigger than the two-family tent that our two families took camping. Flagpoles were spaced evenly along the walk, and the tents were reflected in strange shapes within the shiny silver of the poles, like girls in yellow and green and orange dresses at a carnival house of mirrors. Atop the mirrored poles, flags from every nation represented at the Special Olympics popped their colors in the summer wind, and all of them blew in the same direction.

Billy gave us the grand tour of Olympic Town. It was all for the price of the special admission of being special. There were tents with video games, penny arcades, Ping-Pong, and pool. NASA had set up an educational tent about the space program, and the state had provided a nature tent, complete with fish, small animals, and wildlife posters. There were ice cream tents, soft drink tents, snow cone tents. There was a huge tent with a stage where several musical groups performed daily; and there was a photography tent in whch the Olympians could have their picture taken with a celebrity.

"Why don't you get your picture taken with that movie star, Billy?" I asked when we entered the Kodak photography tent.

"I already had my picture taken with somebody, Harold," Billy answered. "I did it this morning and put the picture in my suitcase, under my underwear so nobody will touch it."

"Did they take your picture with that movie star over there?"

"No, Harold. My picture is with a man who smiled a lot and patted me on the back."

"A politician?"

"I don't remember his name, Harold," Billy said. "Wait a minute, Harold. I remember now! I didn't put the picture in my underwear in my suitcase. I put the picture in my underwear that I got on." Billy reached down in his drawers and retrieved a folded photograph, which he presented to me.

I couldn't believe what I saw in the photograph. Standing next to Billy, his arm around my best friend's shoulders, was Ace Arken, the best quarterback in professional football, and my favorite player in the NFL. "Ace Arken!"

I exclaimed. "The guy in this picture is Ace, the Spaceman, Arken!"

"Is that Ace Arken, Harold?" Billy asked, pointing at Ace Arken's picture.

"That's him."

"Who's Ace, the Spaceman, Arken?" Billy asked.

"One of the astronauts, I guess," Kate said.

"He isn't an astronaut," I said. "He's the best quarterback in football. They call him the Spaceman because he can throw a football almost into outer space."

"Wouldn't that make him Ace, almost the Spaceman, Arken?" Kate asked, smiling.

"Girls!" I said.

"Girls!" echoed Billy.

We continued our tour of Olympic Town, walking from tent to tent, watching the kids watching cartoons, jumping in the Dragon Space Jump, playing miniature golf. There was something different about Olympic Town, something special, and about halfway through the tour, I discovered what it was: everyone was smiling.

When we arrived back at the dormitory, we lingered around on the front lawn for a few minutes. There was hugging going on everywhere, so much hugging that it got a little embarrassing. Billy, the hugger of huggers, led the pack. One good thing about hugs, though: one good hug deserves another. When I hugged Kate, she hugged me back.

"Don't forget to take a bath, Billy," I said as I walked him to his room.

"I already know to do that, Harold."

"Did I tell you that you're my very best friend?"

"Not today," he answered. "But I already knew."

"Good, Billy."

"I got lots of friends here," Billy said. "Everyone likes me, too."

"I'm glad."

"You know what else, Harold? They all want me to show them how to play cards."

"That's great, Billy."

"But do you know this, Harold? They tap on my door in the morning. They come to wake me up every morning. Ain't that a kick?"

"That's a real kick," I said, smiling.

"Hey, look everybody!" a kid called from down the hall. "Billy's back."

"Billy's back?" another kid asked, and within seconds, there were at least ten kids huddled around their friend and mine.

"I sure did miss you, Billy," one said, giving him a hug.

"Want to play cards, Billy?" another asked.

"Let's play Let's Go Fishing in the Clear Blue Lake Where the Ducks Swim and There Ain't No Hunters, Billy," a kid with an English accent said.

"No," another kid said. "I want Billy to teach me how to play poker again."

"Poker?" I asked.

"Don't tell Mommy," Billy whispered.

"I didn't know you knew how to play poker," I said.

"These kids don't know that I don't know," Billy whispered again. "My poker is a lot like Let's Go Fishing in the Clear Blue Lake Where the Ducks Swim and There Ain't No Hunters."

"Sounds like Go Fish has had a few additions to its title, Billy."

"Yes, and ain't it a kick, Harold?"

When I left Billy in his room, there were kids scattered all over the floor, asking Billy questions about cards and sheriffs and Dracula and bicycle jumps. When Billy spoke, his friends listened. I realized that my friend was a leader among his peers, that he was growing up, and it made me happy. Who knows? Maybe he wasn't the only one who was growing up.

Chapter 16

I didn't get to spend much time with Billy the next three days because his schedule was filled with workouts in the mornings and special activities in the afternoons and evenings. For the first time in his life, he spent most of his free time away from me. Each time I saw him over the final three days of the Special Olympics, I noticed that he had changed a little, had grown a little: and still he came to me with open arms and with puckered lips that I was seldom quick enough to avoid.

Although Billy was not around very much, time passed very quickly for me at the Special Olympics. There were events to watch practically every minute of every day, and there was plenty to do at night with Kate. We went swimming every night; we went to the movies twice; we played miniature golf once.

The nights were fun; but the most fun were the days, watching six thousand winners competing in the summer games. The most exciting day, of course, was the third and final day of the Special Olympics, the day Billy's event was scheduled to be run. So far, it was the hottest and most humid day of the Louisiana summer, and I was sweating like a turkey on Thanksgiving eve from walking from one event to another that morning. Billy had never run in such humidity, and it worried me.

An hour before Billy's event, Kate, my parents, Billy's parents, and I met Billy at the track stadium. Everyone wished Billy luck in the race and patted him on the back. When it was time for Billy to locate his coach on the field, everyone went into the stands but Billy and me. We lingered behind a few moments while I gave him some last-minute instructions.

"Remember, Billy, sit in the shade until it's time for you to warm up."

"Okay, Harold."

"Also, cut your warm-ups by fifty percent. You don't need to go through the entire routine when it's as hot as it is."

"Okay, Harold. I will, Harold. What's fifty percent, Harold?"

"Just jog halfway around the track instead of all the way. That should do it. And do half as many sit-ups. Ten sit-ups one time instead of ten sit-ups two times."

"Okay, Harold."

"No, you'd better do fifteen sit-ups. That's ten sit-ups

and then five more. Yes, do fifteen sit-ups, but don't strain yourself."

"Okay, Harold."

"And practice your starts the same as usual. You need more work on your starts."

"Okay, Harold."

"And do all of your stretching exercises, Billy. Do all of them. Don't cut them short."

"Okay, Harold."

"And whatever else you do, please, please, please remember to wear your ankle weight."

"Okay, Harold."

"It goes on your right ankle, Billy. Remember that. The ankle weight goes on your right ankle."

"Okay, Harold."

"And whatever else you do, remember to . . ."

"Harold?"

"What, Billy? Is something wrong? You aren't sick, are you?"

"I'm getting the butterflies. I can feel them flapping around the inside of my stomach."

"That's okay, if they're not really bad, Billy. They aren't really bad, are they?"

"The more you talk, the worse they get."

"What?"

"You're making me real nervous, Harold."

"I am?"

"You're making me think that I won't do good in the race, Harold."

"Oh, no, Billy, don't think that. You're going to do just fine. You're going to run great."

"Then why are you scared?"

"Scared? I'm not scared. I'm just a little nervous, that's all. Actually, I'm a lot nervous. I'm more nervous than I've ever been in my life, except for the time the car almost ran over you."

"Are you mad at me, Harold?"

"Of course I'm not mad at you, Billy."

"You were mad at me when the car almost ran over me."

"I know," I said, "and I'm sorry. But I'm not mad at you now. I'm mad at myself for making you nervous."

"Don't be mad at yourself. I'm not that nervous anymore. I'm going to do just fine, just you wait and see. Now, you just calm down and take it easy, Harold. Everything is going to be okay. You just wait and see." Billy patted me on the back, and I could almost see him growing.

"I think you're absolutely right. I think you're going to do just fine."

"Thanks."

"Listen carefully, Billy," I said, and I grabbed his shoulders. "I'll always be somewhere all of the time. If you want to be somewhere else, I want you to be wherever that is; but if you want to be with me, I want you to be right here. We're a team. We're best friends. We're blood brothers through a common fall, and no matter where we are, we'll be together."

I don't understand the power of emotions, and because I don't understand it, I'm frightened by it sometimes. Sometimes, though, I just let it have its way: like that day at the Special Olympics when I kissed Billy flush on the mouth.

"Boy oh boy, Harold," Billy said, wiping his mouth with the back of his hand and pushing away from me, "somebody might see you doing that."

"Sorry, Billy," I said, smiling.

"That's okay, Harold. Are you going to cheer for me?"

"I'm going to be the best cheerer in the stadium."

I was the best cheerer in the stadium, even though I cheered silently practically the entire race. We had excellent seats, close to the track and near the finish. I watched Billy walk onto the infield and go through his warm-up routine. He'd remembered the string of special instructions I'd given him.

I looked at his right ankle and saw that the ankle weight was strapped in place. He took three practice starts from the blocks, and his rear was too low in all three. Suddenly, an official was positioning the eight boys who were going to run the 400-meter race, and my heart really started pounding. Billy had drawn lane three, which wasn't as good as one or two, but a lot better than four through eight. I chewed on my lower lip and wiped the sweat from my brow.

"Relax," Kate said, biting her lip. "It'll all be over in a little over a minute."

"All that work for something that'll take only a little over a minute," I said.

"It's great," Kate said. "It's great."

I said nothing. The butterflies were doing a number on me, and I didn't want to open my mouth.

"Runners, take your marks!"

All eyes were on the runners.

"Get set!"

The stands were silent.

"BAM!"

The stadium erupted into cheers! It was Billy's best start of his career, but the kid in lane two had a better one. By the time Billy had reached the first curve, he had increased his lead over the boy in lane one and had passed the boys in lanes four through eight; but the boy in lane two was in front of everyone, including Billy.

Out of the curve and into the backstretch, the 400-meter run was shaping into a race between Billy and the kid in lane two. Billy's ankle weight seemed to be doing its job without a problem. He had begun to match the pace of the kid in lane two stride for stride. All the way down the long backstretch, the leader's cleats threw cinders across Billy's legs. It was a close race. Billy stayed in second place, waiting for the right time to pass. The far curve was coming up fast, and I knew that Billy knew that he would have to wait for the final kick in the homestretch to take over first place.

Billy made his move as soon as he came out of the

final curve. His timing was perfect. The leader didn't see him coming until it was too late, and Billy was into his final kick before the kid who shared the lead with him was into his. What a race! It was promising to be the best race of the International Summer Special Olympics Games, and my friend Billy was half the cause of it all.

Billy pulled ahead a little, but the kid next to him pulled up even again. Both of them were calling on every ounce of their energy, every piece of their will to win the gold. I knew Billy's feelings because I had been there; and when what happened, happened, I knew Billy's frustration because I had been there, too.

The tape was in sight sixty or seventy meters down the track, and the kid next to Billy leaned forward slightly, hoping to gain a little momentum from the move. Instead of gaining momentum, however, the kid swerved a little to the right and stumbled. His foot stepped into Billy's lane and came down hard on Billy's leg. Cleats slashed into my friend's flesh and cut into the canvas of his ankle weight.

There was no immediate change in positions on the track. Billy and the kid next to him fell off balance for a second, but they recovered and resumed their fight for first place. Two, maybe three, strides later, however, Billy began to lift his right leg a little higher than his left. No one even noticed at first, except his two coaches in the stands.

"What's going on?"

"I don't know," Kate said. "Billy's leg is up to its old tricks."

"The kid in lane two must have torn his ankle weight," I said. "The lead weights must be falling out with every step Billy takes."

Billy's right leg went a little higher than his left leg with every stride he took, and soon it was shooting into the air as high as it did when he wore no weight at all. The kid next to him was not next to him anymore, and Billy began to fade farther back into second place. I watched in silence as my friend struggled toward the finish line with his uneven stride, and then the inevitable happened. Billy stumbled and fell face first into the piercing cinders, sliding along the track for two yards before stopping. He lay there as the silver passed him by, and the bronze, and fourth place, and fifth, and sixth, and seventh.

"Get up, Billy," I whispered. "You can make it."

"Get up, Billy," whispered Kate. "You've got to finish."

There were hundreds of people in the stands that day, and all of them were shouting for a particular favorite. The roar was deafening, and I really don't think that any of the runners could have distinguished the screams of their fans over the screams of someone else's. Of course, what I think really didn't matter that day. What really mattered was what Billy heard. Billy told us later that he heard his two coaches somewhere in the stands telling him that finishing the race is the only thing that really counts.

"Finish, Billy," shouted Kate.

"You can do it, Billy," I screamed, "just you wait and see!"

When Billy picked himself up off the cinders, I wished immediately that he had stayed down and waited for help. The penetration of the cleats into his leg had been deep, and he was washed in blood from his right knee to his right track shoe. The cinders had scraped and scratched his flesh from his head to his waist, and his hair was matted with sweat and cinder dust. Billy was hurt.

I heard Billy's mom gasp, and I felt the tears welling in my eyes. "You've done enough, Billy," I whispered. "Please stay where you are."

Billy ignored me. Placing one stained shoe in front of the other, he began to walk toward the finish line. After a few steps, he began to walk a little faster, and a little faster still. Ten meters shy of the finish line, Billy broke into a jog; and his fans—hundreds of them—broke into cheers, shouts that would have rocked Madison Square Garden. With a smile on his face, he crossed the finish line and threw his fans a kiss that hit them smack on their hearts.

Billy was helped off the cinders by two volunteers who walked him to a grassy area a few yards on the outside of the track and sat him down. A doctor kneeled beside Billy and began to sponge away the dry blood and the debris from the track that had imbedded itself in his skin.

We rushed out of the stands, the six of us, and stopped at the gate that separated the track-and-field area from the spectators. The six-foot-high fence was locked, but the gatekeeper unlocked it for Mom, Dad, and Billy's parents. The gatekeeper made Kate and me wait outside.

The sick feeling in the pit of my stomach that I had felt when Billy was almost run over by a car returned when I watched him being carried from the track stadium on a stretcher, followed by his dad and his mom, who had a handkerchief to her eyes. I really thought I was going to be sick; but I fought the urge because my knees were so weak that I figured I would buckle face first into whatever it was I had eaten for lunch, and I made it a policy never to eat the same meal twice. I grasped the fence to steady myself. I watched my parents walking toward the gate, and I tried to read their thoughts through their expressions. I looked for sorrow and pain, but all I saw were Mom and Dad and nothing more. Their composure was remarkable.

"His cuts are deeper than they looked from here, aren't they?" I asked my parents as they returned. "He cut through a main artery or something, didn't he?"

"Calm down a little, son," Dad said. "Billy is going to be just fine. A lot of dirt got into the cuts and scratches, so he's going to the campus infirmary to get cleaned up and have his wounds dressed. Also, the doctor thought it best that he return home with us rather than go home on the bus. Questions?"

"Will Billy get to attend the Special Olympics closing ceremonies tonight, Mr. Smith?" Kate asked.

"He'll be there," Dad answered. "We'll all be there."

"When may I go to the infirmary?" I asked.

"Billy's parents are with him," Mom said, "and no other visitors are allowed in the room. Billy wanted you to go with him, too, but the doctor wouldn't allow it. They're going to meet us at the closing ceremonies tonight."

"But Mom . . ."

"I know, Harold," Mom said, placing an arm around my waist. "You're worried about him, but he'll be fine. I promise he will."

Chapter 17

Billy and his parents joined us in Tiger Stadium late that evening as the soccer finals between Chile and Louisiana, the last event of the Special Olympics, were being played. Billy hobbled up the steps to our section as though he were shackled in chains. He was scratched, bruised, and cut, and I imagine every muscle in his body ached. Sadness saturated his face as he approached our row of seats. After the greetings and the hugs, he sat down next to me; and I knew he had been crying.

"Don't be so sad, Billy," I said, my arm around his shoulders. "I'm very proud of you. You finished the race when most people would have quit. Finishing, Billy, is what really counts."

"I know, Harold," Billy replied, "but ain't it okay to feel sad when you didn't win and you knew you could?"

"Yes. It's okay to feel sad."

"Well, I guess I better go now," he said. "I got to sit with my team way over there 'cause we're going to do another parade after the game is over."

"Okay," I said. "I'll see you after the closing ceremonies."

"Bye, Harold," and Billy started down the steps at a snail's pace, moving his legs as if the weight of the world were on his shoulders.

"Billy," I called after him.

"Yes?"

"I'm going to wave to you in the parade."

"Thanks, Harold," he said, and he tried to smile.

The closing ceremonies began promptly after the final event of the games had ended. The special athletes filed from the stands, paraded around the infield, and joined one another on the football field. I spotted Billy as our state's delegation passed in front of our section of the stadium, and I waved to him with my good arm and my broken one. But Billy didn't wave to me or anyone else. He just followed the person in front of him as the parade continued.

Eunice Kennedy Shriver spoke to the gathering of athletes and reminded them of something everyone in the stands already knew: they were all winners. The girl who had lighted the Flame of Hope at the start of the games ascended the steps again that evening to extinguish the flame. Across the stadium, the Special Olympics flag was lowered, not to be flown again until the next International Summer Special Olympics Games. The reviewing stand was emptied of its stars, the special athletes left the field, and the Special Olympics were over.

"We're supposed to get Billy at the north gate," Billy's mom said. "He'll be waiting there with his teammates and coaches."

"May I go get him?" I asked suddenly. "I have something to give him, and I need to give it to him before he leaves the stadium."

"It's fine with me," Billy's mom said.

"Can you find the car, son?" Dad asked.

"I can find it, Dad."

"Be careful," Mom said as I stood to leave.

"What are you going to give him?" Kate asked.

"Something I just thought of," I said. "Something special."

"I'll see you at the car," she said, smiling.

I took three steps at a time going down the stairs and easily took the lead down the exit ramps. When I came to the ground floor, I asked directions to the north gate, which was the next gate around the stadium. Throwing a "thanks" over my shoulder to the person with directions, I ran to the north gate as fast as I could.

The red-and-white uniforms of Billy's team were easy to spot, but spotting Billy in all that red and white was not as easy. I searched the gathering of athletes one time, and then I yelled. "Billy!"

"Harold!"

"Over here, Billy!"

"I'm coming, Harold!"

"Come with me," I said when he emerged from the crowd.

"Where're we going?" he asked as I led him back into the stadium.

"We're going onto the field."

"What for?"

"You'll know soon enough," I said. "Just follow me."

Billy and I made our way back into the stadium, through the box seats section, over the fence that separated the stands from the playing field, and onto the grass of the field. I grabbed Billy's hand and pulled him quickly to the empty circle on the field, where the gold, silver, and bronze medals were awarded after each event. As the stadium was emptying around us, I led Billy to the tallest of the three boxes inside the circle of winners.

"What's going on, Harold?" Billy asked as he stepped upon the pedestal reserved for gold medal winners.

"Billy, you are a true Olympian," I said, looking up at him. "You finished your race when just about everyone else in the entire world would have quit. You are a special person, and you deserve a special Olympic medal, a medal that no one else in the entire world has."

With those words, I reached inside my shirt and pulled the necklace that Billy had given me years before over my head. Spot's old dog tag dangled from the chain as Billy lowered his head, and I placed the medal around my friend's neck. I shook Billy's hand and kissed both his cheeks. "I congratulate you, Billy. You are an example to everyone everywhere. Wear this medal with pride because you deserve it."

"But Spot's medal is your most favorite thing in the whole wide world," Billy said.

"That's okay, Billy," I replied. "You're my most favorite person in the whole wide world."

"I love it, Harold," Billy said. And he kissed me smack on the mouth while the spirits of seventy-five thousand loyal fans looked on.

I slept soundly the night of the closing ceremonies. Billy, bandaged and bruised, slept next to me while Kate slept only inches away in the room next door. If I dreamed at all during the night, I don't remember it, and I awoke the next morning to the sound of a familiar voice.

"Hey, Harold," Billy whispered. His mouth was pressed against my ear, and when he spoke, it felt as if someone had shoved an air hose clear down to my eardrum. "Why are you still sleeping?" he said, his voice echoing through the corridors of my mind.

"What?" I asked, turning my head, sticking my finger into my ear in an attempt to force the trapped air back out.

"You're not supposed to pick your ear, Harold."

"What?"

"You want to see my wound, Harold? Do you want to feel it, Harold?"

"What?" I asked again, still half asleep. I felt Billy take

my finger and place it on something warm and sticky
and . . . "What!" I screamed, sitting up in bed, jerking
my finger from the oozing wound on Billy's leg. I never
wanted to see my finger again. I wanted to boil it in acid.
I wanted to excommunicate it from my hand.

"You'd better hurry and get dressed, Harold," said
Billy. "Everybody's waiting for us to leave for home. But
first wash off your finger, Harold."

The station wagon was packed tighter for the trip home
than it had been packed for the trip going to the Special
Olympics, but because of Billy's gear, we had even less
room to sit. Mom and Dad were in the front seat again;
Billy's parents were in the middle seat; and Kate, Billy,
and I were seated in the back. Clothes, suitcases, bags,
and boxes were stuffed under our feet and behind the
backseat. Everyone was shoulder to shoulder with people or packages, and there was little room to move without rubbing hard against one or the other.

"It's going to be a long trip home," Dad said as he
drove the station wagon away from the motel. I silently
disagreed. I could think of nothing better than sitting in
the backseat for twelve hours with my best friend on one
side and Kate pressed so close to me that her body numbed
my skin on the other. I eased my arm around the back
of the seat, and Kate laid her head against my shoulder.

"It's kind of sad, isn't it, Harold?" Kate said.

"Leaving?"

"Yes, leaving. I could've stayed a month."

"At least a month."

"What about you, Billy?" Kate asked. "Are you sad because we're leaving?"

"I ain't sad," Billy said, "'cause I'm a winner and I'm coming back. Anybody want to play Let's Go Fishing in the Clear Blue Lake Where the Ducks Swim and There Ain't No Hunters, Harold?"

"Sounds good to me," I said. "Anyone know what happened to the cards?"

"They're down here by my feet," said Kate, and she picked them up from the floorboard.

"Better count them," I said. "They've been scattered all over the car for days."

"We're missing one card," Kate said, after counting the stack of cards.

"Look around the floor," I said. "It's got to be here somewhere."

"Do you know what card is missing on the floor, Harold?" Billy asked.

"No. I'm still looking for it."

"I'm smarter than you are!" Billy said. "I know what card is missing on the floor because it ain't missing no more."

"What are you talking about, Billy?" I asked, continuing to search.

"I found the card that ain't missing, Harold."

"You found the card?"

"Here it is, Harold," Billy said, grinning; and I took the king of hearts from the kid with the king of hearts' heart.